The Countertenor Wore Garlic

A Liturgical Mystery

by Mark Schweizer

SJMP<u>BOOKS</u>

Advance Praise for *The Countertenor Wore Garlic*

"Reading this book is like listening to a countertenor in recital. It's an acquired taste, like Dot's holiday beet soufflé or Limburger trifle..."
Richard Kennedy, choir director

"Self-fulfilling prophesy!"
Bill Crowell, Apocalyptic Vice President, End of the World Society

"It's rare that you find a book that you can't put down by an author that should be."
Sir Ron Cooke, Book Reviewer, Mrs. Miggins Coffee Club

"This book is like a lot of opera. Good music, stupid story..."
Dr. Robert Rich, voice teacher

"Great books are lighthouses erected in the great sea of time. This one, however, is more like a dead, vaguely luminescent squid..."
Dr. Richard Shephard, Chamberlain, York Minster

"Schweizer is our Pullet Surprise Winner!"
Chicken Casserole Cook-off, Skunk Valley Days, Saluda, North Carolina

"I just found out that I was switched at birth. Legally, I shouldn't write a review knowing that my baptism records may now contain false information."
Monica Jones, pulpit dancer

"Hey, you other reviewers! If you like this book so much, why don't you marry it?"
Brendon Stanky, 6th grade book reviewer, Pickles Gap Middle School

"Here's a tip! Pack one of these books in with your Christmas decorations. The mice won't go near 'em! Umm ... not that we have mice or anything..."
Donis Schweizer, long-suffering wife

"A clear example of why church music and choir murders go together like possum and parsnips. But why no golfing tips?"
Dr. Bingham Vick, university choral conductor, retired

"A writer for whom the word 'syntax' takes on a whole new meaning and financial obligation..."
Betsy Goree, part-time employee and editor

"Sure I'd love to but I seem to have contracted some attention-deficit disorder and, hey, how about them Packers, huh? So, I won't be able to, yes, could I help you? No, no, I'll be sticking with Verizon, but thank you for calling."
Kathleen Carson, gallery owner

"The perfect size to stick under the corner of your off-center washing machine!"
Art Brown, choir singer

"Anyone can write a book that has a plot. It takes a *real* author to write a book without one."
Mother Ellen Morell, priest, Louisville, Kentucky

The Countertenor Wore Garlic
A Liturgical Mystery
Copyright ©2011 by Mark Schweizer

Illustrations by Jim Hunt
www.jimhuntillustration.com

Published by
SJMPBOOKS
www.sjmpbooks.com
P.O. Box 249
Tryon, NC 28782

ISBN 978-0-9844846-2-1

March, 2011

Acknowledgements
Nancy Cooper, Jay and Betsy Goree, Marty and Randy Hatteberg, Kristen Linduff, Beth McCoy, Mary J. Miller, Patricia Nakamura, Donis Schweizer, Liz Schweizer, Richard Shephard, and Holly D. Wallace

Prelude

In 1936, the Underwood Typewriter Company began construction of a giant-sized working replica of the Underwood Master typewriter for the World's Fair in New York. The enormous machine would take three years to construct and, when completed, would be eighteen feet tall and weigh fourteen tons. The carriage alone would come in at 3500 pounds. When unveiled, it would be billed as "The World's Largest Typewriter." The paper it used would measure nine feet by twelve feet, and the ribbon would be five inches wide and one hundred feet long. After the World's Fair, the huge machine would be moved to the Garden Pier in Atlantic City, New Jersey, where it would attract large crowds who came to view the bathing beauties that Underwood hired to tap-dance on each of the large keys.

Late in 1938, a struggling Los Angeles pulp writer named Raymond Chandler was visiting New York City and stopped in to marvel at the construction of said machine. Having been working on a borrowed and beat-up typewriter, he was in the market for one of his own. For a wordsmith, the typewriter was everything. It was his Stradivarius violin, his Keuffel and Esser slide-rule, his two-pound Sheffield framing hammer. Once a typewriter had been chosen, a writer might keep it for fifty years, eschewing all technical advancements, choosing instead to be faithful to the object that could so easily channel his muse.

Several months later, apparently impressed by the jumbo version he'd seen in New York, and convinced by the Underwood Typewriter Company's admittedly un-seductive motto—*The machine you will eventually buy*—Chandler walked into an office supply store in Los Angeles and spent the princely sum of $109.50 (a sum he could ill afford) on a new No. 5, the most popular typewriter in the world. That summer, he handed the final draft of his first novel to his publisher and the following February held a published copy of *The Big Sleep* in his hands. It was the start of his long, hard-boiled journey.

Raymond and his wife, Cissy, had discovered the lovely coastal town of La Jolla and had been making frequent trips from Los Angeles to the quaint and exclusive seaside village for years. After deciding to rewrite his fifth novel for a third time, and quite tired of hauling the heavy typewriter up and down the quarter-mile stone path to their rental cottage, the author finally took the thirty pound beast to a friend and traded it for a lighter, portable Underwood Noiseless (made for Underwood by the Remington Company) that he could more easily take with him on his excursions. It was the last time he would see the machine that had been such a faithful companion.

The friend, a reporter, moved to Chicago two years later and took the Underwood No. 5 with him. It remained in the offices of the *Chicago Tribune* and was pressed into service throughout the reporter's career to fashion many a story. When the old newshound retired in 1978, the typewriter retired with him, hauled away in the back seat of his Gremlin along with six file boxes' worth of notes and papers. Two years later, he was banging away on this same typewriter, writing his memoirs, when he suffered a fatal heart attack and fell dead on top of the machine.

It was a beautiful funeral, attended by all the good and great in the newspaper community. Someone sang *Seasons in the Sun*, the mid-70's hit made famous by Terry Jacks.

> *Goodbye, Michelle, it's hard to die*
> *When all the birds are singing in the sky.*

Once the vocalist got to the last verse, there weren't many dry eyes in the place, especially since the widow's name was Michelle. Several testimonials were given, one by the editor of the *Trib*, and the faithful typewriter sat on top of the casket for all to admire, a single red rose stuck in the glass keys.

Several weeks after the funeral, the wife decided to go through her dead husband's desk, the desk that had remained off-limits and locked for as long as she could remember. She took a long-handled screwdriver and a hammer and after a couple of whacks, the locks gave way and the drawers slid open. The widow sat in the old wooden chair and read the beginning of his memoirs. There wasn't much—two complete chapters and a few extra pages—so it didn't take her long to discover that her husband's exploits during their time in California included frequent cocaine use, four bisexual orgies, a sordid affair with a well-known B-Film actress—and he hadn't even completed chapter three, the one entitled, "1940-41, The Randy Years." She'd hoped, after first glancing at the chapter heading, that "Randy" referred to their beloved Golden Retriever. It hadn't. After that, she couldn't bear to look at the typewriter and relegated it to the attic where it sat unused and unloved for the next two decades.

Eventually the woman died and the children returned to the house to go through thirty-five years' worth of memories. When they got to the attic, the eldest daughter found the typewriter in a dusty corner. Upon cleaning it, she found half a piece of paper stuck in the housing. On this paper was typed the following:

> This typewriter belonged to Raymond Chandler
> and was used to write his first four novels.

That anonymous piece of provenance and an accompanying letter by Raymond Chandler thanking his reporter friend for exchanging "that hulking piece of junk" for the more portable Underwood Noiseless was enough for the auction house to accept it as genuine, issue a certificate of authenticity, and advertise it in an online auction—an auction I happened to see.

Now, some years later, the typewriter sat on my desk. It had taken a lot of cash (which I had in abundance) and a few weeks' work by my new friend Max in Philadelphia to get everything in tiptop shape. Max fixed things, typewriters in particular. He'd had to replace the carriage return lever (badly bent when the reporter fell dead across the keys), clean the innards, grease the gears, change the oil, rotate the tires, and whatever else typewriter technicians do. He did a great job. It worked like new.

I hadn't seen the letter from Raymond Chandler since it wasn't part of the auction package, so I was a bit put out when I found out from Max (another Chandler aficionado) that my hero hadn't used this typewriter to write *all* his works of fiction. I soon got over it. The first four novels were plenty. *The Big Sleep* might well be my favorite and it was Chandler's first. *Farewell My Lovely, The High Window,* and *The Lady in the Lake* followed. All works of genius as far as I was concerned, and quite enough for me. I ruminated over a well-chosen phrase from *The Big Sleep* that had been first typed on this machine and typed it again, looking at the characters on the heavy 24 lb. bond as if seeing them for the first time, seeing them as Raymond Chandler might have seen them in 1939.

```
Vivian is spoiled, exacting, smart and quite
ruthless. Carmen is a child who likes to pull
wings off flies. Neither of them has any more
moral sense than a cat. Neither have I.
```

I typed another line.

```
I don't mind your showing me your legs. They're
very swell legs and it's a pleasure to make
their acquaintance.
```

Once I sat down at the typewriter, chomped on an unlit Cuban *Romeo y Julietta,* donned Raymond Chandler's actual fedora (another acquisition of an aspiring writer with too much disposable income), and flipped on the green-shaded banker's lamp, I was in another world. That I'm the Chief of Police in our little township of St. Germaine, North Carolina, was a fact that melted into the background. My avocation as part-time organist and choirmaster at St. Barnabas Episcopal Church faded as well. My wife, my friends, my whole world, disappeared into one of those fogs that envelops Humphrey Bogart and Ingrid Bergman as they stand on the runway, hands shoved deep into the pockets of their trench coats, the propellers of the getaway plane slowly spinning in the background.

"You'll regret it. Maybe not today, maybe not tomorrow, but soon, and for the rest of your life," I heard a voice say.

"We'll always have Paris," I replied. "I'm no good at being noble, but it doesn't take much to see that the problems of three little people don't amount to a hill of beans in this crazy world."

"What the heck are you talking about?" said Meg.

"Huh?" I snapped out of the trance and looked around the room. Meg was in the kitchen doorway eyeing me with suspicion.

"Are you talking to yourself again?"

"Umm. Nope," I said, but after a long courtship and three years of marriage, Meg was not easily fooled.

"I was saying," she continued, "that I think you may regret inflicting any more of your detective stories on the choir. Maybe not today, but soon. Marjorie is starting to review them for the church newsletter."

"A good writer does not fear reviews," I said, taking the cigar out of my mouth and waving it in defiance. "He welcomes them. He embraces them."

"Hayden Konig," Meg said sternly, "may I remind you that you're not a good writer. You're a terrible writer. Literary reviews are not your friend. You should fear them. You should cower before them like Lindsay Lohan at a drug rehab facility."

"Hey, that's not bad! Can I use that?" I typed Meg's one-liner onto the page in front of me.

"No, you may not," said Meg. "If you do, it's plagiarism, pure and simple."

"Never stopped me before," I muttered.

"Besides," said Meg, "I spent the better part of the afternoon thinking it up."

My attempts at detective fiction were becoming legendary, at least in my own mind. I had begun with *The Alto Wore Tweed* and worked my way through the choir—baritone, tenor, soprano, bass, and mezzo—before branching out to include the diva and the organist. I typed these stories on the faithful typewriter (hoping for a little of the Chandler magic), and put them, one chapter at a time, into the choir folders. I was proud to say that some of my best work had been recognized in a national competition. Never mind that it was a competition for the worst sentences ever written.

I pulled the piece of paper containing my warm-up efforts out of the typewriter, stuck it into the desk drawer, rolled a new piece of foolscap behind the platen and typed:

The Golovshchik Wore Gabardines

Meg walked up and read it over my shoulder. "A golovshchik?" she said, pronouncing the word carefully. "What's a golovshchik?" She set a beer on the desk.

"Ah," I said. "Thanks for the suds and I'm glad you asked. A golovshchik was the singer in an early Russian church choir whose role consisted of performing solo verses or the initial phrases of hymns. He carried a stick, presumably for whacking unruly choristers."

"So he was sort of a cantor?"

"Well, yes. A cantor."

"Then why not call him a cantor?"

"Alliteration," I replied. "Besides, *The Cantor Wore Gabardines* doesn't have much of a ring to it."

Meg nodded. "Yes, you're right about that. You haven't done a countertenor yet."

"I haven't done a castrato, either. How about *The Castrato Wore Cutoffs*? I find that the title works on so many levels."

"No." Meg scowled at me, but I was immune to scowls.

"Okay," I agreed. "*The Cantor Wore Culottes*?"

"Funny," said Meg, "but no one knows what culottes are anymore."

"Chintz? Crinoline? Chaps?"

She tapped a finger against her chin as she thought. "Use the countertenor," she said. "And don't worry about the alliteration." Her visage became abruptly austere. "But if anyone ever asks," she sniffed, "I avow no knowledge of this conversation. In fact, I categorically deny any involvement in your literary efforts." She turned and walked back toward the kitchen. I watched her go for a moment, enjoying the view. Meg couldn't fool me. She was beginning to like this stuff.

I pulled the paper out of the typewriter, wadded it up and tossed it into the old metal trash can that was quickly filling up beside the desk. Then I rolled in another sheet and typed:

```
The Countertenor Wore Chintz
```

Nope. I tore the page out, crumpled it and tossed it in the bin. Close but no cigar. And I needed a cigar. Also a beer. I picked up the bottle. Murphy's Irish Stout. I took a swig, replaced the discarded sheet, then sat and thought for a long moment.

"By the way, have you decided what you're going to be playing?" called Meg. "On your Halloween recital? Georgia was asking. She wants to put a flyer in the bookstore window."

"Yep," I called back. "I think I'm going to accompany a silent movie. Probably *Nosferatu*."

Meg poked her head back into the room. "Never heard of it," she said. "Is it good?"

"It's a 1922 film starring Max Schreck as the vampire Count Orlok," I said. "Very spooky."

"Sounds great," said Meg. She disappeared back into the kitchen. I heard the oven door bang shut and the smell of lasagna, Italian spices, and garlic bread wafted through the house.

Halloween.

The typewriter clattered, seemingly of its own accord, and I looked down at the page.

```
The Countertenor Wore Garlic
```

It felt right. I was off and running.

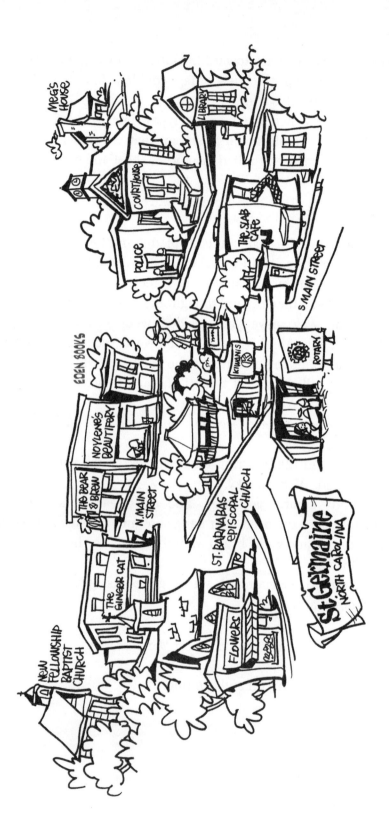

Chapter 1

Sing, o ye muses, of Noylene's wrath on Triple Coupon Day at the Piggly Wiggly.

"This is a *trapesty*!" Noylene yelled, loud enough for all the other customers in the grocery store to turn and gawk in amazement. "Amelia Godshaw, I demand to see the manager!"

Annette Passaglio, next in line behind Noylene, suddenly decided that she could use another twelve-pack of anything handy and backed her cart down aisle two, pretending she hadn't been in line at all. Annette was one of the grand-dames of St. Germaine and wouldn't think it seemly to stand calmly in line behind an irate, vocal, and possibly insane customer. She stopped backing up when she got to the display of toilet paper, then picked up a single roll of Charmin and pretended to read the instructions on the back, her free hand fidgeting nervously with her pearls as though they were a rosary.

Meg and I were checking our groceries with Hannah at the next register over. Hannah was doing her best to ignore Noylene, but I could see her bristle.

Hannah, Grace, and Amelia were the self-proclaimed "checkout girls" at the Pig. To characterize the three women as "girls" was a stretch since they hadn't seen girl status for sixty years. They all lived together, were fast friends, and since a robbery at the grocery store a few years ago, were all known to be packing heat. Roger Beeson, the long-suffering manager, tried to label them "sales associates," but they wouldn't have it. "We're the checkout girls," said Hannah, "and don't you forget it."

Amelia growled. "Noylene Fabergé-Dupont-Hog or whatever the heck your name is this week, you keep your voice down, or I'll do it for you." She pulled her pistol out from under the counter just far enough for Noylene to glimpse the grip and part of the barrel, then slid it back out of sight with a hard look at her customer. Noylene was not intimidated. She spun and pointed a finger at me.

"You see that?" Noylene yelped. "She pulled her gun on me!" She turned her fury back to Amelia. "And his name is McTavish, not Hog. Hog is his first name. Hogmanay McTavish."

"Why don't you shut your yap?" muttered Amelia in a low voice, but loud enough for all of us standing at the registers to hear.

Noylene turned to me again and barked, "I demand you arrest this harlequin! She can't be drawin' down on innocent people in a grocery store."

"I believe you mean 'harlot,' dear," corrected Grace. "A harlequin is something totally different." She turned and addressed Amelia. "She meant to call you a *harlot*."

"*Harlot?*" said Amelia, her eyes going wide with shock at the accusation. "*Harlot?* You don't even know what a harlot is, you... you... *bucolic bumpkin!*"

"Let's calm down, ladies," I said. "Amelia is certainly not a harlequin, er... harlot, and Noylene can certainly not be considered bucolic."

"Dang straight," huffed Noylene. "I got all my shots last month. Now what about that gun?"

"I didn't see a thing, Noylene," I said. "I was thumbing through the *People* magazine." I looked at Amelia and offered her my second best law enforcement glower. "I'm sure that these three ladies are aware of the consequences of threatening customers with a firearm."

Amelia humphed. Grace and Hannah shifted their gazes to the ceiling as though tracking a dragonfly that might have flitted through the automatic doors.

Roger Beeson came running from his office when he heard the disturbance. He was a congenial fellow, but couldn't seem to keep any help at the Piggly Wiggly except for an almost vaporous stock boy named Clem, and the three ladies who didn't really need the money and were happy to work for minimum wage. Winter or summer, Roger always wore a white shirt with the sleeves rolled up, a tie, dark slacks, and a red vest with P. Wiggly's picture screen-printed on the right breast. On the left side of the vest, a garment which at one time may have buttoned neatly but now no longer stretched across Roger's ever burgeoning belly, the manager's name and title was embroidered. One of his shirt tails was untucked and he had the harried look of a manager who, on October 21st, had just phoned in the order for his fall pumpkins. He nervously smoothed a damp wisp of black hair across the top of his scalp.

"What's wrong, Noylene?" he said, exasperation evident in his voice.

"It's Triple Coupon Day, ain't it?" said Noylene. "I've got coupons."

"We're not giving you cash back," said Amelia with a snarl. "Says so right in the ad."

"No, it don't," answered Noylene, triumphantly slapping her copy of the *St. Germaine Tattler* onto the conveyor belt. "Lookit here. Last month the ad said 'no money back.' Not this month. You forgot!"

Roger picked up the newspaper and skimmed the ad. Then he sighed heavily, handed the paper back to Noylene and addressed Amelia.

"She's right. I forgot. Go ahead and give her the money."

"Forget it!" said Amelia.

"I'm the manager," hissed Roger. "You're causing a scene and customers are leaving the store. Give her the money!"

Amelia crossed her arms in defiance. "Nope. Everybody knows that on triple coupons, you don't get money back. Free stuff, sure, but no money back. That's just the way it is."

Noylene waved the paper under her nose. "Doesn't say so..."

"How much is it?" asked Roger.

Noylene pointed to a stack of items that hadn't been sacked yet that included a gallon of charcoal lighter fluid, five bags of off-brand dog food, and a large assortment of feminine hygiene products. "My triple coupons all add up to $63.76. The bill is $58.45. You guys owe me about nine dollars!"

"It's $5.31," said Amelia, "but we're not paying."

Roger dug into his pocket and came up with a hand full of bills. He counted out six ones and pushed them into Noylene's hand.

"You don't even have a dog," Amelia said to Noylene, her disgust at Roger's submission evident.

"Well, I've got me some dog food," said Noylene, waving the bills under Amelia's nose, "and six dollars to boot. Maybe I'll just go and *buy* me a dog since y'all are paying me to take this food home."

Amelia gritted her teeth but didn't say anything.

Noylene put on her nicest smile. "Maybe you could put these in a paper bag for me."

"I'm on break," said Amelia. "Do it yourself."

Amelia locked her register and stomped off toward the break room. Roger stepped behind the counter, bagged Noylene's purchases and set them into her shopping cart.

"I'll be back in a little while," Noylene said cheerfully, as she pushed her cart toward the exit. "As soon as I print up some more of them coupons. Y'all know you can just get 'em right off the Internet?"

"We think it's the hormones," said Hannah after Noylene had gone. "Her baby's what? Ten months old? She's been in and out of here like a wild woman for the past six weeks. It's driving us crazy." Hannah ran our two sirloin steaks across her scanner. "You have any coupons?"

"Nope," I said.

"Nope," said Meg.

"Hmm. You have your Piggly Wiggly discount card?"

"Nope," I said.

Meg shook her head and proffered an apologetic smile.

"We can also accept your Food Lion discount card if you have one of those," said Hannah hopefully. She lowered her voice. "Or I can let you use mine..."

"We insist on paying full price for these steaks," I said. "It's our anniversary."

Megan Farthing Konig and I have been married for almost three years. Three years this Thanksgiving to be exact, but October

21st was another one of our anniversaries. Not the anniversary of our first date. That was July 15th, the day that Meg went zipping past my '62 Chevy pickup in her Lexus and I was forced to detain her with a dinner of knockwurst and sauerkraut, grilled to the sounds of J.S. Bach on the stereo. July 15th, eight years ago.

October 21st was when she took me home to meet her mother.

Ruby, Meg's mother, had been living in St. Germaine for five years or so prior to Meg's arrival and I'd remembered seeing her around town, of course, but even in a small village of 1500 or so people, unless you ran afoul of the law or needed a police chief's particular services, there was a pretty good chance that I might not have made your acquaintance. Besides, Meg's mother is a Baptist. Baptist folk do not co-mingle with Episcopal folk unless provoked. In St. Germaine, Episcopalians will get together with Methodists (a common heritage), Lutherans (a common distrust of Papal authority), Presbyterians (a common love of mixed drinks), and Unitarians (because they'll drink anything), but Baptists? No sir. Baptists keep to their own kind.

The reason that I remembered seeing Ruby around town is that, although she is now in her seventies, she is a striking woman. Tall and statuesque with silver hair that still showed hints of black, she is an older version of Meg—same dancing gray eyes, same beautiful smile, same knockout figure, same wicked sense of humor. Meeting Ruby on October 21st wasn't particularly memorable, but it was another date Meg and I could celebrate, and we enjoyed celebrating.

Unlike her mother, Meg is not a Baptist. She is an Episcopalian. So Episcopalian that she'd been the Senior Warden of St. Barnabas for the past three years. It was a position she'd hold only for a couple more months. The church tried to elect her again, George Romanski nominating her and citing the age-old St. Barnabas motto, "If it ain't broke, don't fix it." This motto of course, flies in the face of the other, more prevalent St. Barnabas motto, namely, "If it ain't broke, have a committee tinker with it until it is," and "If it *is* broke, leave it alone and maybe it'll fix itself." Meg declined the nomination.

As Senior Warden, Meg had done a marvelous job overseeing the rebuilding of St. Barnabas after the famous Thanksgiving fire that had consumed the 1904 structure. She also worked very well with our current priest, Gaylen Weatherall, but she feared, like all of us, that Gaylen wouldn't be around for too much longer. Finding yet another priest was a task that Meg wanted no part of.

Gaylen had been called as rector of St. Barnabas, but then had been elected Bishop of Colorado and moved to Denver. It was a position she decided to vacate when her aging father, whom she was caring for, developed emphysema and couldn't deal with the altitude of the Mile-High City. We welcomed her back to St. Germaine with open arms since she was much loved, and because we hadn't had good luck with priests since her departure. Gaylen's father had gone to his eternal reward this last April, and now the Right Reverend Weatherall was on the short lists of at least two episcopates that we knew of. She'd be a sitting bishop again in a matter of months if not sooner. Whether Gaylen left or not, Meg had informed the vestry that she'd be retiring as Senior Warden come the new year.

"That'll be $34.56," said Hannah, dropping our steaks, a couple of sweet potatoes, and some salad fixings into a bag. "And Happy Anniversary!"

"Thanks," I said. I handed Hannah two twenties and pocketed the change.

A couple of minutes later we were pulling out of the Pig in my '62 pickup and heading for the hills. I could afford better than the old truck. I could afford anything I wanted. As fate and luck might have it, I was quite the tycoon; this thanks to an invention I sold to the phone company at the height of the cash boom of the 90s and the proceeds having been shrewdly handled during the recent financial crisis by my extremely savvy broker, Meg. Oh, yes, she'd made me a bundle. As she so succinctly put it, "You've got more money than Tammy Faye's housecat. Why don't you buy a decent truck?" I didn't buy a decent truck, because this one was perfectly good. Better than good. The most expensive thing in it was the sound system. That and the Glock 9 under the seat. I kept an identical pistol in the organ bench at the church. I've always found that tenors can use a bit of encouragement.

I turned on the stereo in the truck and the sounds of Mussorgsky's *Night on Bald Mountain* filled the cab.

"I recognize that," said Meg, "from Disney's *Fantasia* movie. I remember that I especially like the ending."

"That ending's not on this recording," I said. "When he made *Fantasia*, Mr. Disney stuck Schubert's *Ave Maria* onto the end of it, and had it sung by some supplicants going to church to make it not so scary. All nuns and church bells. This is the original. Halloween at its finest."

"It certainly sets the right mood," agreed Meg.

We swung onto the highway and drove up in the direction of our cabin. We called it a cabin. It was anything but. Nestled on two hundred acres, one of the rooms, currently the library, began life as a log cabin. Daniel Boone's granddaughter and her husband had built it in 1842 and I'd had it taken down, log by log, moved to the property, and reassembled. The rest of the house had a mountain cabin feel to it, but in reality had more in common with some of the upscale dwellings in Blowing Rock and Boone than with the mountain cabins that were tucked away in the hollers of Watauga County. In the three years that we'd been married, Meg had put her stamp on the house as well, including renovating the kitchen, redoing the bedrooms and the cabin library, and adding a garage, something my old pickup had never seen the need for. Her new Lexus, however... well, that was a different story.

"Who's minding the store this weekend?" asked Meg.

I knew what she meant. The third weekend in October was prime leaf peeping season in St. Germaine and, weather permitting, the biggest tourist weekend of the year. The two weekends leading up to Christmas were second and third maybe. Since this was destined to be a glorious weekend, meteorologically speaking, the town would be packed. Heck, it was already packed, and this was only Thursday.

"I'm off tomorrow. Nancy and Dave both have weekend duty. I'll check in Sunday after church, but unless there's a problem, I won't be hanging around."

We took a tight curve and Meg slid across the seat and bumped up next to me.

"You did that on purpose," she said.

"Yep. It was my move in high school. If the girl didn't slide back to her own side, I knew she liked me."

"Hmm."

***

We drove down the road that constituted our driveway, across a pasture and up to the house, and were greeted by Baxter, watchdog extraordinaire. He barked his basso greeting, once, twice, then made for the kitchen door where he waited for us, tail wagging, in anticipation of spreading more of his thick white, black, and tan fur across the house. With winter coming, I would have expected that Baxter might keep a bit more of his coat, nature's hedge against the bitter months that were right around the corner. I was mistaken.

Meg let him in and he raced for his place under the kitchen table, skidded to a stop, banged into a chair, regrouped, and made himself as inconspicuous as a one hundred ten pound dog can be while waiting for an escaped dinner morsel dropped accidentally on purpose. He'd wait there for ten minutes or three hours. Didn't matter to him. If he sensed that there was food to be served, he was in his place.

"I'll cook these potatoes and make the salad," said Meg. "Give me about an hour and then you can put the steaks on the grill."

"Good deal," I said. "I'll be at the typewriter."

I'd put some CDs next to the Bose stereo system before we'd left this morning and now loaded them into my brand new 100 CD changer and turned it on. Halloween music. Music that goes bump in the night. The sounds of Grieg's *In the Hall of the Mountain King* filled the house.

Meg stuck her head out of the kitchen and yelled, "Could you turn that down? You're scaring the salad."

I turned the volume down—moderately down—because I felt that Halloween music should, at the very least, rattle your skeleton, then turned my attention to my new opus. I put on my fedora, turned on the banker's lamp that cast a yellow glow across the paper already in the typewriter, and began.

The Countertenor Wore Garlic

It was a dark and stormy night, although Tessie, the one o'clock weather girl on Channel Two, had nasally predicted a clear and starry night, but was once again dead wrong, chiefly due to her education (Meteorology for Blondes), her inability to read a tele-prompter, and her current preoccupation with the ever-burgeoning hope that this fellow she'd been hearing about, Doppler Radar, would ask her out on a date. The wind howled through the city like wind might do if it was howling and not just blowing; but I guess "blowing" would be more accurate because, quite frankly, "howling" is exaggerating the point since all the wind was really doing was making the kind of whistling sound your grandfather might make while trying to pronounce his S's after dropping his teeth in the dog's water bowl, but surely "blowing" could not describe the darkness and storminess of this particular night as it (the wind, not the night) moved like a howling, whistling thing across the dank (and by dank, I mean damp) cityscape.

I'm a detective. A liturgy detective, duly baptized by the bishop, absolved by the diaconal ministers, licensed by the archdeacon, and happy to take everyone's money. Sure, I specialized. There were other gumshoes out there that were happy to specialize as well--snooping, dirty snaps, sordid, lustful affairs, intrigue, embezzlement and such. Still, that's what I liked about church work. I had all that and religion besides.

The music ended and the opening strains of the fifth movement of Berlioz's *Symphonie Fantastique* filled the house. Meg stuck her head out of the kitchen again.

"A bit morbid this evening, aren't we?" she hollered, struggling to be heard above the music. "How about some nice Couperin harpsichord sonatas?"

"You wish!" I yelled back. "Can't talk. I'm on a roll."

Usually I was scrambling like a five-legged cockroach at an Irish step dancing competition. For the past six weeks, though, business was dead, and I don't mean the good kind of dead where there's a body and I can charge two C-notes a day plus expenses. I mean the bad kind of dead where there's nobody dead. I had a nut to make and the rest of the squirrels weren't taking candy corn.

The economy was so bad that when Marilyn went to her weekly exorcism and couldn't pay, the priest repossessed her. I had to tell her to take a permanent vacation. A secretary whose head spins all the way around tends to put a client off. Now I was down to calling a few low-level canons, bishop wannabes who were hiding past careers as music evangelists and I had the record jackets to prove it. I didn't like blackmail, but I knew these Holy Joes, and I knew they'd throw some shekels my way to bury that vinyl in someone's back yard.

The unmistakable strains of the *Dies Irae* began to rumble in the bowels of the orchestra. Day of judgement, day of wrath. I closed my eyes and let the music envelop me until I felt a hand on my shoulder.

"Time to put on the steaks, Mr. Shakespeare," said Meg. "Or rather, 'Mr. Chandler.' I think you fell asleep."

"Maybe," I said. "Did you turn the music down?"

"Just a hair." She kissed me on the cheek, then, moving her lips to my ear, said in a husky whisper, "Before you grill those steaks, how about putting something a bit more romantic on the stereo? I'll make it worth your while."

Thank you, Harry Connick, Jr.

Chapter 2

The cowbell tied to the door of the Slab Café banged loudly against the glass when I walked in, announcing the arrival of yet another hungry customer. I wiped my dress shoes on the mat inside and looked for Nancy and Dave, whom I suspected would be frequenting the establishment, it being nine in the morning and an hour into their shifts. I didn't have to look far. The Police Department had a table in the back, complete with a RESERVED sign molded in high-gloss red and engraved with white letters. Nancy had had the sign made and no one, not even Pete Moss, the owner, dared to take it off the table. The cherry red of the hard plastic matched the decor of the Slab to a tee. Each of the tables was covered with a red and white checked vinyl table cloth, and the chairs, although wooden, had seats covered in a lovely red Naugahyde. This fabric choice extended to the six booths along the side wall and to the upholstery of the four chrome stools that sat in front of the aluminum trimmed, white linoleum counter. The floor was also tiled in a checkerboard pattern, eighteen inch squares of black and white. The counter top and each of the tables were adorned with the requisite ketchup bottles, salt and pepper shakers, small bottles of Tabasco sauce, and sugar shakers. A refrigerated pie case leaned against the far wall. There were also menus. We didn't need the menus.

"What are you doing here?" asked Nancy as I walked up to the table, having made my way through a raft of customers, all eating breakfast as though it were their last meal. "You're off today."

"Breakfast," I said. "Meg had some business, so I came into town for breakfast." I pulled out a chair and sat down. "How are things in the constabulary?"

"No problem," said Dave with an affable grin. "We have everything under control."

Nancy Parsky and Dave Vance were the other two-thirds of the SGPD. Dave had been moved from part-time to full-time status after it had become apparent that Nancy and I couldn't police the town by ourselves—especially from the beginning of October through Christmas. Corporal Dave did most of the office work, answering phones, typing reports, and such. He and I both dressed in civvies although mine tended toward work khakis and L.L. Bean flannel shirts during the cold seasons. Dave was more J. Crew and worked the chinos and light blue button-down motif, although when the weather turned cold, he favored Icelandic sweaters. Dave was in his mid-thirties, blond, and in reasonably good shape. He'd had a schoolboy crush on Nancy Parsky, off and on, for the past seven or eight years. Nancy, on occasion, returned the favor.

"What's the special, Noylene?" I asked, as she poured my coffee. We didn't order coffee. Coffee was a given.

"Meatloaf," said Noylene, then held up her hand to stop the next words out of my mouth. "Yes," she said slowly through clenched teeth. "Meatloaf. Don't ask me why. I don't know. Meatloaf and eggs with a side of cheese grits. It's some bee got under Pete's bonnet. He read about this restaurant in *Southern Living*. Savannah or somewhere. They serve meatloaf and eggs for breakfast."

"Anybody ordering it?" I asked.

"*Everybody's ordering it!*" said Noylene, then lowered her voice to a whisper. "These tourists are just plain crazy. You give them weird and they lap it up like it was caviar on a cat plate."

"I ordered it," said Nancy with a shrug. "Sounded kind of good to me."

"Not me," said Dave. "I'm having pancakes."

"*There's* a surprise," said Nancy.

Nancy's a crackerjack cop. The only reason she hadn't moved on to a bigger police force in a bigger town is that she liked it here and I made it worth her while to stay. Lieutenant Parsky had been courted by Greensboro, Asheville, and Charlotte, not to mention the smaller towns around St. Germaine. She'd been offered the chief's job in Lenoir and Roanoke and the assistant PC job in Boone. She turned them all down. When on duty, Nancy was always in her uniform, cleaned and pressed with creases in all the right places. Her sunglasses were clipped to her left breast pocket just above her badge, and her pad and pen always handy in the

24

other. Her nails were clipped short and she wore no jewelry except a triathlete black-banded watch. When outside in brisk weather, the 9mm Glock on her hip was partially hidden by her leather bomber jacket. Otherwise, it was always in plain sight. She was an excellent shot. Her brown hair, as usual, was tied into a tight bun at the back of her head. She didn't wear a cap. Nancy could be quite attractive when she chose. On duty she appeared formidable. Tourists who received speeding tickets from Nancy rarely tried to talk their way out of them.

"I'll have the meatloaf," I said. "Why not?"

Me? I came to St. Germaine nineteen years ago at the behest of my college roommate. The town was looking for a highly qualified individual and although my Master's degree was in music, my third degree in criminology was the deciding factor for the mayor. "You can give 'em the third degree," he quipped as he signed my contract.

The mayor at the time was none other than my college roommate, Pete Moss, so the fix was in. Pete was an old hippie, still reading Carlos Castaneda, sporting a ponytail, wearing Hawaiian shirts with his wire-rimmed glasses, and nurturing a long-standing aversion to undergarments. He was pulled down from his mayoral sovereignty three years ago in a hard-fought (and some said "hilarious") campaign against Cynthia Johnsson, our town's only professional belly dancer, and now spent his time hunting, and running this fine eating establishment. He looked at his political loss philosophically. He looked at Cynthia philosophically, too, but since she frequently waited tables at the Slab, this philosophizing turned to lust pretty quickly. She was a belly dancer after all, and Pete, although a two-time loser in the marriage department, knew a good thing when he saw it shimmying. They'd been an item since the eve of the election. He now perceived his civic duty to be much like that of Rasputin: the evil power behind the throne.

Noylene sighed, wrote the order on her pad and set off for the kitchen. "I'll bring it all out together," she said without looking back.

"She seems sort of on edge," said Nancy, her gaze following Noylene into the kitchen.

"Hormones," I said, as I took a sip of my coffee. Nancy snapped her head around and gave me the stink-eye.

"Or so I've heard," I backtracked quickly. "Yesterday, she was fighting with Amelia at the Piggly Wiggly trying to get six bucks back on triple coupons."

"You don't get money back on triple coupons," said Dave. "Everybody knows that."

"She knew it," I said. "And she certainly didn't need the six bucks."

"Lucky Noylene didn't get shot," said Dave. "Amelia's a stickler. One time I tried to sneak thirteen items through her ten-item-or-less line. She reached under the counter, but I switched lines real fast."

"It's not hormones," Nancy said, her detective radar beeping like a smoke detector with a bad battery. "You guys are idiots. It's something else. Why's she working the morning shift anyway? This is the biggest weekend of the year. She ought to be over at the Beautifery."

Noylene Fabergé-Dupont-McTavish was, by all accounts, a wealthy self-made woman. A few years ago, she'd started *Noylene's Beautifery, an Oasis of Beauty,* taking advantage of her God-given talent of granting beauty to others less fortunate than herself. She'd married her cousin, Wormy Dupont, and perfected the Dip-N-Tan, a contraption invented by her son D'Artagnan, in which her customers could hang from a trapeze and be lowered into a vat of tanning fluid. It took a few months to get the formula right, and for a while her plus-sized customers resembled giant mutant sweet potatoes, but soon the women in St. Germaine all looked as though they spent every weekend, summer or winter, on the beaches of Jamaica. Added bonus: no tan lines. Above the Dip-N-Tan was a sign that read

I am dark, but comely, O ye daughters of Jerusalem.
Song of Solomon 1:5

26

Noylene was nothing if not biblical and the Dip-N-Tan was a rousing success. Unfortunately, Wormy couldn't stick around long enough to enjoy the fruits of the Beautifery, the Dip-N-Tan, or even the profits of his own venture, the Bellefontaine Cemetery (affectionately known to the locals as "Wormy Acres"), due to his murderous tendencies and well-founded jealousy concerning his lovely wife. He was currently doing twenty-five-to-life in the Big House for giving in to the green-eyed monster and whacking Russ Stafford in the head with a giant rock during the Bible School's reenactment of the Stoning of Stephen. After his conviction, Noylene sold the cemetery, filed for divorce, married Hog, and never visited Wormy, not even once.

"Here y'all are," said Noylene, returning with an armload of plates. She set them absently on the table and headed back into the kitchen.

"That's not right," said Nancy.

"Yeah," said Dave. "She forgot to fill my coffee cup. And she gave me your meatloaf."

"These pancakes look good, though," said Nancy as she poured the hot maple syrup over the stack.

"Hey! Wait a minute... I don't like that much syrup!"

"It's okay, Dave," said Nancy as she lifted a forkful of flapjacks to her lips. "You'll enjoy the meatloaf just as well."

The fourth chair at the table scooted out with a scrape and Pete plunked himself down.

"Busy morning," he said, "and we haven't even started." He pointed to the plate glass window that constituted the front wall of the Slab. Since I'd come in ten minutes ago, there were six customers inside the door waiting for a seat to open up, and a waiting line on the outside clear past the window. Beyond the line of hungry people and across the street, Sterling Park was already bustling with folks coming in for the weekend. Parking was at a premium and if the library lot was full, the best bet was down the road at the grocery store or maybe the bank. Of course, you might get lucky and manage a spot on the square if you happened to be in the right place at the right time.

"Aw, jeez," whined Dave. "I hate meatloaf."

There were four eateries in the vicinity if you counted the coffee shop behind St. Barnabas. Holy Grounds, our Christian Coffee Shop, was run by Kylie and Biff Moffit. They'd had a rough first year, but were now back into the busy season and looking profitable. The coffee was good and they sold an assortment of muffins and other baked goods to go with it. The Ginger Cat was diagonally across the square. It was an upscale, snooty luncheonette owned and run by Annie Cooke, but she didn't open for breakfast. The Bear and Brew around the corner served pizza and beer, but not until eleven. It was no wonder the Slab did a brisk business.

"I have a delivery for you in the back," Pete said to me. "Kent Murphee brought it by early this morning."

"Kent Murphee?" said Nancy between bites of Dave's pancake breakfast. "The coroner? What is it?"

"Two big boxes of dead baby squirrels. I've got them in the walk-in freezer for you."

"You're kidding," said Dave, who'd been poking around his meatloaf before finally deciding the cheese grits and eggs were edible even though they'd been touching the edge of the gravy. "What for? A Halloween prank?"

"Probably the lunch special," said Nancy. "Squirrel head gumbo."

"I love squirrel head gumbo," said Pete. "Grew up on it. 'Course they say now you're not supposed to eat the brains. Some of the squirrels have that crazy cow thing going on."

"Creutzfeldt-Jakob disease," said Nancy. "East Tennessee just had another outbreak."

"Yeah, that's it," said Pete. "Mad squirrel."

"They're for Archimedes," I said. "I supplement his diet. Mice in the summer, baby squirrels in the winter. Don't want him to go hungry."

"Do owls like meatloaf?" asked Dave, pushing the piece of meat to the edge of his plate. "I'd rather eat squirrel brains than meatloaf."

28

Noylene walked up to the table, whisked up Dave's plate and put a fresh platter of pancakes down in front of him. "We could hear you whining all the way back in the kitchen. Here y'all are. Eat up."

"Noylene, I love you," said Dave happily.

"Welcome to the club, Noylene," said Nancy. "Dave loves anyone who will feed him."

Noylene patted him on the head like a puppy, then turned her attention to me. "Hey, I've got a question. Are those your baby squirrels in the back?"

"Yep."

"I'm only asking 'cause I could sure use a handful of 'em for a stew I'm cooking up. There's nothing better than a few tender sugar-babies to flavor the stock."

"Nope. Sorry, Noylene. They're for Archimedes."

"How's that old fella doing, by the way?" asked Nancy. "I need to come by and see him."

"He's just fine."

Archimedes is a mostly tame, mature barn owl. He is predominantly white and has a wingspan of about two feet, which allows him ample space to float through the main living space of the house without obstruction. He's been part of the family for the past six years, coming and going as he pleases, thanks to an electric window in the kitchen. Baxter ignores him for the most part since he has no interest in meals-on-wings. I feed Archimedes quite regularly, but that doesn't stop him from hunting on his own. In warmer weather, we'll see him in the top of a big oak next to the house, pulling pieces off an unwary rabbit, a field-mouse, or even the occasional snake. During the winter, the owl spends a great deal of time during the day perched on the head of my full-sized stuffed buffalo, preferring the warmth of the house to the naked wind in the trees. Most nights, winter or summer, he's up and away.

"Hmm," said Noylene. "Too bad. Hog had his teeth set for some squirrel." She exhaled heavily from between pursed lips.

29

"Well, I've got to head on to the Beautifery. We've got appointments all day starting at ten. I've got to go open up."

"What's wrong, Noylene?" I asked. "You feeling all right? You look plumb worn out."

Noylene's shoulders slumped. "I jes' can't get any sleep. Lil' Rahab's got the croup and I haven't been to bed since Methuselah was a boy."

"What'd Dr. Dougherty say?" asked Nancy.

"She's got him on some medicine. It helps his cough some, but he don't sleep more than an hour at a time. I gotta hold him or he's not happy."

"Where is he now?" I asked.

"Hog's got him," she said. "This morning I just had to get out of the house. He's bringing Rahab up to the Beautifery. I got a room set up in the back. The girls and I take turns walking him."

"By the way," I said, "did you go back to the Piggly Wiggly with some more coupons?"

Noylene smirked. "Nah. I jes' wanted to rattle Amelia's cage. I've been waitin' for months for Roger to screw that ad up. Amelia and me... well, we go way back. About twenty years ago, on the day before Thanksgiving, she up and stole the last turkey in Watauga County right out of my grocery cart when I left it for a minute to get a can of cranberry sauce and some pecans. *Right out of my cart!*"

"That's quite a grudge," I said.

Noylene wagged a finger at me. "I'm sorry," she continued, "but when something's in your cart, it's your own rightful property unless you put it back on the shelf or leave the store for any reason. That's the law. Says so in the Constitution."

Pete nodded his agreement. "I'm no Constitutional scholar, but I believe she's right."

"Oh, that was just the beginning," said Noylene, her eyes brightening just a bit. "We been at it grammar and prongs ever since."

"We are defined by our enemies," I said.

Noylene looked puzzled, then glanced toward the front door as she heard the cowbell clank. "I guess. Anyway, here's Cynthia. She's picking up my shift."

We looked toward the door and saw Cynthia Johnsson making her way through the crowd gathered at the entrance of the café.

"Thanks for the pancakes, Noylene," said Dave. "You're a peach!"

Noylene accorded him a wan smile, tossed her apron into a laundry basket behind the counter, and disappeared through the kitchen. My phone buzzed and I took it out and looked at it. A text from Meg.

"You know how to text?" said Nancy. "When did this happen?"

"I don't really know how to text, but I know how to read. They're two different and mutually exclusive skill sets. See?"

I held the phone up so Nancy could see it.

"I just pick the phone up and read it. It's amazing."

"But you can't actually *send* a text?" asked Dave.

"I guess I could if I wanted to," I replied, "but why bother? I just pick up the phone and call."

"Maybe the person on the other end doesn't want to talk to you," said Cynthia. She now had her apron on and was filling coffee cups around the table. "With a text, you can say a few quick words and be done. You don't have to chat about the weather and such. You can get off the phone quick."

"I do that now," I said.

"It's true," agreed Nancy. "He does. No chitchat. So what did Meg want?"

"See, that's another thing. As soon as your phone dings, everyone wants to know what someone wants."

"Ooo," said Nancy, blowing across the top of her coffee and then taking a slurp. "Touchy."

I sighed. "I'm supposed to meet her and Bev and Gaylen at the church. Right now. Big meeting."

"Not good news I'll bet," said Pete.

"No sir," I said. "I suspect not."

Chapter 3

St. Barnabas Episcopal Church, the oldest church in St. Germaine, was founded in 1846. It has an unusual history including two devastating fires and some genuine miracles. The first of these (both the fire and the miracle) happened in January of 1899. When the parishioners showed up for services on that icy winter morning, they found their church building in smoldering ruins. They were shocked and saddened, of course, but this shock soon gave way to wonder and then to praise as the congregants gathered around the altar of St. Barnabas—an altar that should have been destroyed in the fire, but had instead been discovered outside the church in the snow, all the communion elements in place. The consensus of those looking upon the miracle was that the heavy altar had been transported outside the inferno by angels. The marble top of the table had been replaced a few years ago, but that didn't seem to bother anyone. The legend of the angelic intervention was gospel in our part of the country.

The second church building was constructed in the early 1900s. It was a beautiful stone and wood church built on a familiar design. The nave, or main body of the church, was in the shape of a cross. The transepts, near the front formed the arms of the cross. The high altar (after having survived the fire) was placed on the dais in the front, a smaller Mary altar in a transept, with the choir and the pipe organ in the back balcony. The steps to the choir loft were in the narthex, the entrance to the church. The sacristy, where the clergy put on their vestments and where communion was prepared, was behind the front wall. Two invisible doors in the paneling behind the altar offered access to the sacristy from the nave. It wasn't a large structure. Seating was limited to about two hundred fifty.

That building burned to the ground at Thanksgiving three years ago.

I exited the Slab Café, crossed the street and made my way across Sterling Park, loose leaves rustling underfoot with every step. The dark red doors of St. Barnabas were standing open, as was our tradition in good weather at least, a welcoming gesture to all those tourists who found themselves milling around St. Germaine and in need of a brief respite.

There were two miracles that occurred on the fateful Thanksgiving weekend that St. Barnabas burned. First and most importantly, no one was hurt despite the fact that the church had been full of people attending a Thanksgiving pageant. Added to that, there was no other damage to the town of St. Germaine, even though the church sat on the town square in close proximity to many other structures. This was thanks, in large part, to the St. Germaine Volunteer Fire Department. They couldn't save the church—that much was clear to everyone watching—but they could try to contain the fire, and contain it they did with a mix of heroics, teamwork, and many muttered prayers.

The second miracle was the one that the town still talks about, at least those folks who believe in angels.

On the morning after the fire, it was discovered that while everyone was occupied with the chaos that was raging on the town square, the altar of St. Barnabas—the holy table that had been part of the fabric of the church since 1842—had been moved from the burning building into the park across the street. When the congregation gathered together in the frosty morning air, intent on having a service of thanksgiving, they found the altar, upright and unscathed amongst the brightly colored leaves, the communion bread and the wine sitting on the marble top.

The rebuilding took nineteen months and the new building looked almost exactly like the old. The dilapidated old house on the lot behind the church, left to St. Barnabas when the owner died, had been torn down and the lot turned into a garden, a lovely addition that had been landscaped to take advantage of the mature maples, oaks, poplars, and dogwoods that, in summer, formed a canopy across the almost-one-acre lot, and in autumn, afforded as colorful a view behind the church as Sterling Park did in front.

I entered the church through the side door and heard voices coming from Gaylen Weatherall's office almost immediately. Marilyn, the church secretary, was sitting glumly at her desk, pretending to push some papers around. She nodded toward the adjoining office and I knocked on the door jamb, then entered when Gaylen motioned me in.

Meg was sitting in one of the fabric-covered wingback chairs facing Gaylen's desk, drinking a cup of coffee, the picture of calm. Bev Greene, the parish administrator, was in the other wingback, close enough to the big desk to drum her fingers across the dark mahogany. There were four folding chairs set up in the office behind the two upholstered ones, but the other three people besides myself—Billy and Elaine Hixon and Carol Sterling—chose not to sit. The air of resignation was palpable.

"Well," started Gaylen, "I guess we all know why we're here."

No answer. I glanced at Elaine. She looked as though someone was about to punch her.

"I've been elected to be the Bishop of the Diocese of Northern California."

"Aw, crap!" said Billy. "I knew it."

"I asked them to hold off on the announcement until I informed the parish."

"Well, the cat's out of the bag now," I said.

A puzzled look crossed Gaylen's face.

"Meg sent me a text while I was at the Slab informing me of the meeting," I explained. "I'm afraid that conclusions were jumped to. By now, the word is on the street."

"Can't you keep your texts to yourself?" asked Bev.

I raised my hands. "It wasn't my fault. The phone dinged."

Meg graciously changed the subject. "When do you leave?" she asked Gaylen.

"This will be my last Sunday," said Gaylen. "I'm not going to drag this out since we've all gone through this before. I'm welcome to start my new position as soon as I want."

"Oh, that's just great," said Carol. "What are we going to do for a priest? All Saints' Sunday is coming up and Advent is right around the corner."

"I shall not leave you comfortless," said Gaylen with a smile. "Everything is planned through Christmas. You'll be happy to know we already found a supply priest. He's waiting in the parish hall to meet everyone."

"Anyone we know?" asked Bev.

"I don't think so," said Gaylen. "Although I understand that he has family in the area. Maybe a brother. He's a priest in Scotland, here on a three-month sabbatical. His diocese in Aberdeen wants to plant a sister church near Grandfather Mountain. There's quite a Scottish heritage up this way, you know. He'll be moving here full-time when the diocese gets the church up and running."

"So he's starting a new church from scratch?" asked Billy.

"That's the plan," said Gaylen. "A Scottish Episcopal church. Until then, he's certainly willing to act as a supply priest for St. Barnabas. At least for the next three months, or until the search committee can fill the position."

"How did you find him?" asked Bev.

"It was almost like a miracle," answered Gaylen with a smile. "The very day I found out I'd been elected bishop, he knocked on my door and introduced himself and told me he'd love to stand in if ever I was unavailable. He had his Scottish Episcopal ordination papers in his hand. A quick call to Bishop O'Connell and it was a done deal."

"Hang on," I said. "He has a brother in town?"

"I believe so," said Gaylen, puzzling for a moment. "I think it must be a brother."

"Well," said Billy. "Let's go meet this fellow."

"What's his name?" Meg asked, suddenly wary.

"Fearghus McTavish," said Gaylen. "He's a colorful character. I think you'll all get along just fine. He's got a wonderful Scottish brogue and he wears a kilt."

Meg lost her color and looked over at me. "Oh my," she managed. "Well, I guess... for a little while..."

"You know him?" asked Gaylen, suddenly concerned.

"No," I said. "But I think we might know his brother."

***

Fearghus McTavish stood at attention in front of the fireplace. His hands were clasped behind his back and his neck bulged with muscles that seemed to belie his current profession as a minister of the gospel. Most priests that I knew boasted a less formidable physique.

"Maybe that's not Hog's brother," whispered Meg as we gaped, astonished, at the massive figure standing before us. "Doesn't look anything like him."

Hogmanay McTavish, known to us as Brother Hog, was a corpulent man, a short and plump tent-evangelist with one defining feature: one of the finest "comb-overs" that any of us had ever seen. His one long strand of silver hair sprouted behind one ear, swung across his brow, circled his head once, then twice, then terminated in the middle of his tufted nest, fastened to his bald pate with a piece of toupee tape.

The man in front of us bore no resemblance to Hog whatsoever, being over six feet tall, muscular, hairy, and built like a professional wrestler. He was wearing a kilt—shades of red, light blue, and black plaid—in what I assumed was the traditional McTavish tartan. His kilt-hose, heavy woolen socks that stretched over his massive calves, were shades of gray and had the nubby look of handmade apparel. He was wearing a navy jacket over a starched white shirt and a striped regimental tie. The coat tugged against the bulk of his shoulders. I knew the look. A cheap, off-the-rack wool blazer for a physique that was anything but off-the-rack. His hair was thick, coppery-red, and cut short, and he sported a close-cropped beard and a huge imperial mustache. He had the ruddy complexion of a redhead and a hard edge in his green eyes that glowered at us from under eyebrows that looked like ginger-colored ferrets. He tried to give us what might have passed for a smile, although it was difficult to tell, his yellow, gap-toothed attempt being mostly hidden by his walrus whiskers. The effect was rather staggering. Staggering and terrifying. This was a man who obviously had little occasion to smile and the allowance, once made, disappeared quickly from his visage.

"I'd like to introduce Father McTavish..." started Gaylen.

"Vicar," corrected the Scotsman in a heavy brogue that rattled out of his mouth through clenched teeth. "I am a minister of the Gospel, not some primate's bootlicker. I prefer to be called Vicar."

Noon of us were aboot to aergue.

Chapter 4

I got to church early. I didn't usually practice on Sunday morning before church, but on this particular morning, I had my hands full. The title of the offertory anthem that was printed in the bulletin was a piece called *Sing Unto God*. It was a great anthem—one of the choir's favorites by Mr. Handel from his oratorio *Judas Maccabaeus*. Still, it was a toss-up whether enough altos would show up to make a go of it. The anthem began with altos singing the theme and only three had been to Wednesday night rehearsal. Truth be told, they weren't the three I would have liked to see sitting in those chairs. I could double them up with some of the sopranos at the beginning, but after that, we were toast. Too many runs, too much exposed singing. I had a back-up plan, though: another Handel anthem, also on a paraphrase of Psalm 96, this one in two parts and easy enough to put together in a few minutes if my worst fears came to fruition.

Seated at the organ console, I had to assume that we'd do the first, more difficult one and it had more than enough black notes to persuade me that it would be a good use of my time to woodshed it before the choir showed up.

I'd made it through the first couple of pages when I heard the first footfalls stomp up the wooden steps to the loft. I expected Marjorie Plimpton, one of our tenors who was almost always twenty minutes early. She'd drop her grandkids off at Sunday School, grab a cup of coffee in the parish hall, and head for the choir loft to refill the flask she kept under her chair before anyone else showed up. Her "refill" bottle was in the organ case stuck behind one of the larger pipes and I didn't dare ask what it contained. That I occasionally was there when she replenished her supply didn't bother her. I was mildly surprised, therefore, when I glanced up from a cadence and saw not Marjorie but Bev Greene. I stopped practicing and waited for her to speak.

"I think that we and Bishop O'Connell have made a terrible mistake," she said.

"Really?" I feigned surprise. Bev ignored me.

"As church administrator I feel that I can offer a well thought-out opinion. He's horrible."

"The bishop?"

"The priest. McTavish."

"Horrible in a good way?" I asked.

"Horrible in a horrible way. He refuses to help with the communion service as long as Gaylen's celebrating. He's made it quite clear that he won't be served by a woman. Nor will any congregants once he is in charge."

"Perhaps they have different customs in Scotland."

Bev looked nervous. "He'll probably just stand there at attention for the entire service. The only thing he consented to do is to say the prayer after the offertory."

"I'll bet he just wants to see how the service flows since he'll be taking over next week."

"He growls to himself a lot. I think he's what you might call a Calvinist Anglican with strict Scottish Presbyterian leanings."

"Sort of flinty, eh?" I said. "A bit rigid?"

"In a word. He told me he prefers to use the 1549 edition of the prayer book in his daily devotions and, if he had *his* way, we'd be using it for services."

"Hmm. Ol' King Henry's prayer book? Is that allowed?"

"No," said Bev miserably. "But the old 1928 version *is* allowed if he gets the bishop's permission."

"Has he?"

Bev shrugged.

"So," I said, "no more snuggly couples-counseling? No codependent nurturing support groups? No twelve-step programs?"

"The only twelve-step program he'll be participating in is the eleven running steps he takes before he kicks you in the kiester."

"We'll manage," I laughed. "It might only be for a little while. He might be just the impetus the search committee needs to move quickly."

"I believe he'll be wanting us to switch to one of the Scottish metrical psalters."

"Could be worse."

"And we'll be getting fire and brimstone in the sermons."

"Probably good for us."

Bev eyed me with suspicion. "You're enjoying this, aren't you," she said. "You're one of *them*."

***

The choir gathered in the loft thirty minutes before the service. My plan was to rehearse the anthem and go over the service music. It was a plan that seldom succeeded.

"Hayden's a closet *Manglican*," Bev said to Meg as soon as Meg sat down in her chair. "Did you know that?"

"Manglican?" said Meg.

"Man Anglican. A religiously crazed, male-centered, orthodox conservative who prefers the 1928 prayer book."

"Sure," said Meg with a shrug. "I knew that."

"Before you married him?"

"Oh, yes. Although 'orthodox' is a stretch. He's anything but orthodox. But crazed? Yes, definitely crazed."

"Harumph," said Bev.

"To tell the truth, I rather like the old prayer book, too," said Marjorie. "It reminds me of when I was a girl."

"Totally different," said Bev with a dismissive wave of her hand. "You prefer it because you're old. Hayden prefers it because he's a man."

"Old?" said Marjorie, bristling. "Who's old?"

"I never said I preferred it," I said. "I just indicated that I shall make the best of whatever situation presents itself." I lowered my voice to a mumble. "Although, now that you mention it..."

"We're using the '28 prayer book?" asked Elaine, joining Meg and Bev in the soprano section. "Are we allowed to do that?"

"Hope so," said Marjorie as she thumbed through her music folder. "Hey! Look! Our new liturgical mystery." She pulled the Psalm for the morning out of her folder, flipped it over and started reading the story I'd copied onto the back.

40

"I hope it's better than the last one," said Martha Hatteberg, one of the Back Row Altos, or BRAs, as they rather liked to be known. Martha was one of those who'd missed the rehearsal on Wednesday and I was glad to see her, thinking we might have a chance at the anthem after all. Seated next to her was Rebecca Watts, happily reading. But there were still seven altos missing.

"Excuse me!" I said. "That last story was rather brilliant."

Muffy LeMieux and her husband, Varmit, came into the loft. Muffy dreamed of the stage at the Grand Ol' Opry and sang accordingly. She had a signature look that she thought would play well in Nashville—tight angora sweaters, stretch pants, and big, dark-red mall hair that tended to change shades from week to week. Her husband, Varmit, was the foreman down the mountain at Blueridge Furs and didn't sing much, at least as far as I could tell. His job, as he saw it, was to hunker down in the bass section and keep an eye on Muffy. Muffy waved to me and flounced down amongst the sopranos.

"Georgia said to tell you she can't make it," Muffy said.

Another alto down.

"How about Tiff?" I asked, referring to our unpaid choral intern from Appalachian State.

"Fall break," said Fred May from the back row where the basses sat. "She said she was leaving for the week. Anyway, the basses are all here."

He was right. Bob Solomon, Mark Wells, Steve DeMoss, and Phil Camp joined Fred and Varmit in the bass section. The tenor section, anchored by Randy Hatteberg and Marjorie, had been supplemented by Burt Coley. Burt, who had a degree in music, was employed by the Boone Police Department and took weekend duty whenever he could. I couldn't count him as a regular, but he was here this morning, so I didn't have to worry about the tenors. Of the twenty-eight on the choir role, sixteen were present and all the sections were represented pretty well—all except the altos.

"Where's Sheila?" I asked Steve.

"Asheville," said Steve with no further explanation.

"I can't really sing," said Martha. "I just came to offer moral support. I've got the crud." Rebecca, the only alto left, looked up from her reading, startled.

"Elaine?" I said hopefully. "How about singing in the alto section?"

Elaine shook her head. "No way."

"Bev?"

"Manglican," said Bev accusingly.

I sighed, resigned myself to the easier anthem, and pulled it out of the pile of music sitting on top of the organ.

"This story is okay," announced Marjorie, "but it doesn't go anywhere. There's no plot."

"None of his stories go anywhere," said Meg. "You should know that by now."

"You need to take a writing course," said Muffy. "Over at the college. I took a song writing course last year and it helped me a lot. That's when I wrote my song *Please Bypass My Heart*." She started singing in her country twang. "Please bypass my heart, but don't pull the plug on our love..."

"That's great," I interrupted, "but this installment is just the introduction to the drama. The next chapter will be scintillating and will include many grammatical devices, including meandering conjunctions and itinerant participles."

"Fancy talk for someone who got a 'D' in college English," said Meg.

I ignored her. "Criticism later—now, down to business. We need to look at the Psalm and pray for altos."

"We always pray for the altos," said Elaine. "You know, 'Dear Lord, forgive the altos for their many transgressions...' It's in the St. Barnabas Chorister's Prayer."

"I mean, let's pray for *more* altos," I said.

"A little character development wouldn't hurt, either," said Mark. "Plot and character development. That's what you need."

"I've been saying that all along," said Meg with satisfaction. "Hayden definitely needs some character development."

There was a noisy honk at the back of the choir loft and everyone turned around to see what the commotion was. There, framed in the stained glass window, was Dr. Ian Burch, PhD, the town curmudgeon, with a handkerchief in his hand, wiping his long, glowing, snipe nose. Dr. Burch had several degrees in musicology and owned the Appalachian Music Shoppe on the square, a store that specialized in Medieval and Renaissance period musical instrument reproductions. He lived in two rooms at the back of the store. The Shoppe didn't have many walk-in customers except during peak seasons, but his employee, Flori Cabbage, had told me that they did quite a brisk business through their website. Ian's most arresting features, other than his beak, were his ears, large and prominent, jutting from his small flat head. That he was blowing his nose like a bugle was no surprise to anyone that knew him. Ian Burch was the foremost pine pollen sufferer in the county.

"Hi, Ian," said Mark Wells. "Are you going to accompany us this morning on your nose, or is there a rack-pipe part in this piece?"

"Rauschpfeife," said Ian in his freakishly high nasal voice. "I play the sopranino rauschpfeife."

"There's no rauschpfeife part, I'm afraid," I said.

"I didn't think there was," said Ian. "Otherwise you would have called me. I need to get my singing voice back in shape and I wondered if you could use an alto?"

"Sure," said Rebecca. "Do you know one?"

Dr. Burch sniffed and snorted into his handkerchief again. "I am quite a good alto—countertenor, actually—and have sung in many madrigal and early music venues. As a *chanteur*, I specialize in the works of Gilles Binchois, specifically his chansonnier oeuvre from the 1430s, but I'm also quite versed in the chanson baladée repertoire of Dufay and Machaut. I can audition if you'd like." He cleared his throat and made a high, keening sound.

"No audition necessary, Ian," I said. "Glad to have you. We're not singing anything in Medieval French this morning, but there's a folder sitting on that chair next to Martha. It's Tiff's seat, but she's absent."

A dark look of disappointment crossed his face, but he took the chair and opened the folder.

"Okay, everyone," I said. "Let's try the *Judas Maccabaeus* anthem. And sing it like you mean it."

***

Dr. Ian Burch, PhD, turned out to be one heck of a countertenor and navigated the exposed alto part in the anthem with ease. When we completed the final cadence, everyone turned to him in amazement, then burst out in a cacophony of appreciation and delight. Ian was obviously embarrassed, but gratified at the approbation and honked his thanks. We went through the Psalm and our short communion anthem, a lovely piece titled *When Rooks Fly Homeward* by Arthur Baynon that was one of Gaylen Weatherall's favorites and what would be the choir's musical farewell to a good and much-loved priest. Then the choir made for the sacristy to put on their vestments and take their places for the processional hymn.

The first part of the service went fairly smoothly. Gaylen announced her plans to leave us for the verdant hills of Northern California, but almost everyone had already heard the news. The grapevine of St. Barnabas was nothing if not effective. She said goodbye to the children during the Children's Moment, introduced her replacement, Vicar Fearghus McTavish from St. Drinstan's parish in Old Muke, Scotland, and incorporated her impending departure nicely into her sermon. The only slightly strange business was the obdurate and grim presence of the priest. He stood, ramrod straight, off to the side of the altar, and didn't move at all after he'd assumed his place. He was even more imposing in his clerical garb than he was in his tartans, looking imperial in a long black cassock with two white preaching tabs. We sang the anthem at the offertory and it went splendidly. Ian did a yeoman's job with the alto part and Rebecca, having a section leader she could depend on, followed with fearlessness.

We sang the Doxology and waited for the prayer. Gaylen was at the altar holding both offering plates aloft obviously waiting for Vicar McTavish to bless the gifts. After what seemed an interminable silence, he turned and faced the congregation. Then he raised his arms toward the heavens and prayed, in a tremendous bass voice:

"O most omnipotent, wrathful, and unforgiving Father. Sanctify these unwarranted mercies to us, the lowliest of miserable sinners. Let thy distress at our wanton grievousness be our distress, let thy anguish be our anguish. Make thy servants bow the knee to thy terrible majesty and grovel in the dust like the worms we are."

Meg looked at me, her eyes wide. Every other member of the choir was staring at the Scottish vicar.

"Holy smokes," muttered Bev. "Worms? We are in for it!"

"Turn our rancorous hearts from wickedness," continued McTavish. "Beat our carnal desires and lascivious thoughts from us as with a three-pronged flailing stick and blind us, yea Lord, even as thy servant Samson was blinded with white hot spikes driven into his eyes—yea even this, almighty and pitiless Father, to forfend the wanton blandishments of worldly things and turn our feckless endeavors toward thy continued glory. Amen."

"Amen," muttered the stunned congregation, most of them unable to get the image of white-hot spikes out of their minds.

Vicar McTavish growled. His lips were coated with flecks of foam as he seemed to contemplate, with a certain degree of satisfaction, the prospect of the members of his flock being spit roasted over the eternal bonfire. Then he clasped his hands together, then turned back and faced the communion table. He didn't move again until the clergy recessed during the last hymn. He certainly didn't take communion.

Chapter 5

I was still working the phones when the door to the
office flung open and there she was, her hair whipping
around her head like the tail of a horsefly-crazed
pony--a beautiful pony named Tessie that my sister got as
a Christmas present the same year I got a clock-radio,
not that I'm bitter or anything--and that brings us back
to the weather girl Tessie who was now standing in the
doorway, not looking like a pony at all, but when she
spoke, did turn out to be a little hoarse.

"Urgh," she croaked through lips that were as thin as
her rain-soaked silk dress, her profile, her resumé, and
her probable reason for coming to me. She sauntered
across the floor like Saunterella, the sauntering siren of
Sauntyville, and didn't really need to speak; her wet
dress clinging to each delicious curve said it all: "I'm a
beautiful but vacuous weather girl whose evil stepmother
was just killed by vampire-hunting Methodist assassins,"
or maybe, "Do you know a good dry-cleaner?"

"I need help," she finally squawked in a voice that
had failed to endear her to over fifteen men in three
years. "My name's Tessie. Tessie Turra."

"I know who you are, Doll-face, and we all need help,"
I said, stuffing cotton in my ears, lighting up a stogie,
and eyeing Tessie's assets--assets which, as far as I could
see, and I could see plenty, did not include a checkbook.
"You need help, I need help, even the Archbishop needs
help. Why come to me?"

"I heard you were the best Liturgy Detective on the
block. That, and that you might cut a girl a break if she
didn't have the dough."

I looked at her. "Yeah? And?"

"My evil stepmother..."

"I know all about it. What else?"

She looked at me like a cow just before it's milked, horror and betrayal in her soft, brown eyes. "My sister's undead. She's been unmurdered and I think I'm next!"

I wasn't unsurprised.

"Undead?" said Meg.

"I'm taking advantage of all the vampire stories that are so hot at the moment. Vampires are very in. Georgia's having one of the authors do a signing at Eden Books."

"Ooo, that's a good plan," said Meg, with no little bit of sarcasm. "You'll enrapture all those teens that love a badly written, church music vampire mystery."

"Mock me if you will. I am secure in my aesthetic."

"I think that Halloween music is getting to you. What's playing?"

"Guess."

"I guess Holst. Something from *The Planets*."

I looked up at her from the typewriter. "You're exactly right. That was *Mars, the Bringer of War*."

She gave me a smile that made my socks tingle.

"You're getting pretty adept at this classical music stuff," I said, "but that was easy." I reached for my CD remote, clicked it, and the music changed abruptly. "How about this one?" I asked.

Meg thought for a moment. "*The Witch's Ride* from *Hansel and Gretel*."

I clicked again. She listened, then said, "*Mephisto Waltz No. 1*. Franz Liszt."

"Huh?... what?... you?..."

Meg smiled again and patted me on the cheek, then walked out of the room. I stared for a moment in bewilderment, then turned my attention back to the typewriter.

"Unmurdered, eh?"

"What else would you call it?" she whimpered wanly yet piteously. "She walks the streets all night long wearing shapeless black dresses and biting the necks of Methodists. That's why they're out to get her."

47

I'd heard of these abominations. We all had. Methodists...
No, wait a second. I mean the Vampire Amish. I'd thought
they were just a rumor--scuttlebutt thrown around by the
Mennonite Red Cross to discredit the annual Amish Scouts'
Cookie Sale. Now it seemed as though we were up to our
necks in them. Our long, sweet, swanlike necks.

I grabbed my gun and her hand. "C'mon, toots. I know a
guy who knows a guy."

***

On Wednesday morning Sterling Park was bustling. I'd
stopped by the Holy Grounds coffee shop on my way into town
and gotten a large cup of unpronounceable coffee made with the
droppings of a civet cat on the recommendation of Kylie Moffit,
our local barista. It was on sale for $9.95 per cup, but for the rarest
coffee in the world, Kylie assured me, the price was quite a
bargain. It was usually double that. She had received a big order
and there was some left over. "That's why we're letting it go so
cheap," she explained. "The order is for a special event, but the
customer told us we were free to keep what was left over after he
had what he needed. Nice, eh?"

Cheap or not, at ten bucks a cup, I didn't dare put any cream or
sugar in it as was my custom. I was bound and determined to
drink it straight up.

I sat down on a park bench, hoping to enjoy my midweek
morning splurge as well as the wonderful late October weather
and the activity in the park that characterized small town life here
in the Appalachians. Our little burg was gearing up for the St.
Germaine Halloween Carnival, and Cynthia Johnsson, in her
capacity as mayor, was busy overseeing the installation of booths,
games, and events that would comprise Saturday's festivities.

The carnival was the idea of the Kiwanis Club when it became
apparent that the Rotary Club had a death grip on the town
Christmas activities this year. Usually the Christmas parade and
the Christmas Crèche—our "Living Nativity"—alternated between
the two civic organizations, each club trying to outdo the other.

Unfortunately, in late September, Beaver Jergenson's climate-controlled horse barn had burned down, and Beaver's barn was where the Kiwanis Club stored their Amish-built stable, costumes, manger, lighting equipment, and the rest of their Nativity paraphernalia. So, although it was the Kiwanians' turn to host the Christmas Crèche, it didn't look as though they had enough time to rebuild, revamp, refit, and make it all happen by Thanksgiving. Their stable had been beautiful, a mini-chalet straight from the front of a Swiss postcard that featured carved corbels and brackets, a gabled and thatched roof, exposed beams, painted gingerbread moulding and several balconies; they had been on the cover of *Our State* magazine, for heaven's sake, and they weren't about to take a step backward. If Mary, Joseph, and the baby Jesus had been in the Kiwanians' stable on that first Christmas, they'd have had to use their American Express card to tip the concierge for directions to Egypt.

When Beaver's barn burned down, the members of the Rotary Club had happily volunteered their own crèche, but made it clear that they weren't about to give up their rights to the parade. It was then that the Kiwanis Club brought forth their new idea of a Halloween Carnival, an idea that was quickly embraced by the town council, five of them being Kiwanians, and only four comprising the dissenting Rotarians. That all the proceeds raised from these civic endeavors went to benefit a common scholarship fund that was administered by the Friends of the Library made no difference. It was the competition that mattered.

Cynthia plopped down beside me with an exhausted huff.

"Good morning, Madam Mayor," I said. "How are things?"

"Oh, fine, I guess," said Cynthia. "What're you drinking?"

Cynthia's query was of a professional nature. She not only worked at the Slab, but also at the other two restaurants in town—the Ginger Cat, our expensive, boutique eatery with an unintelligible menu featuring such delicacies as roasted plantain and wood-fired caper sandwiches topped with plum duff couli—and the Bear and Brew, chiefly known for good pizza and twenty-two micro brews on tap. In addition, Cynthia sometimes worked the

49

counter at Holy Grounds, but being one of the two professional waitresses in town, found that she didn't make enough tips at the coffee shop to make it worth her while.

"I think they call it Cat Crap coffee," I said, making a face. "I haven't made up my mind about it yet."

Cynthia laughed. "Kopi Luwak," she said. "Made from partially digested beans that have been redeposited on the fertile earth by the Asian palm civet cat. It's been called the world's finest coffee. I think it's an acquired taste."

"Ten bucks a cup."

"Well," said Cynthia, "you can afford it."

Cynthia was quite a looker, even though now well into her forties. Along with her part-time job as mayor and her full-time waitressing profession, she also found time for her passion: belly dancing. She said it kept her in shape and Pete Moss was happy to agree.

"How's the carnival shaping up?" I asked.

"Pretty well, I think. Booths are starting to go up and we have a lot of interest. The Kiwanis Club is in charge, of course, but the Rotary Club has a ring-toss game with big-ticket prizes."

I took a sip of coffee and tried to decide if it was any better than the seventy-five cent cup of coffee at the Slab.

"Halloween isn't until next Tuesday," I said.

Cynthia ignored me. "Then there's the Daughters of the Confederacy booth. They're selling homemade baked goods." She named the groups and counted them off on her fingers. "Friends of the Library, the Town Council, the Moose Lodge, the DaNGLs..."

"The DaNGLs? What are *they* doing?" The Daystar Naturists of God and Love were our local Christian Nudists, headquartered over at Camp Daystar, formerly Camp Possumtickle, about three miles from town.

"Selling pumpkins, I think," said Cynthia. "The Piggly Wiggly didn't get any in. Never fear, they all promised to wear clothes." Cynthia rummaged through her jacket pockets, then gave up. "I've got a list somewhere. Anyway, I'm not in charge. I was just out here checking to see if everything was going as scheduled. Just for your information, official town trick-or-treating is scheduled for Saturday night after the carnival. Halloween is on a Tuesday this year, and Tuesday is a school night."

"You're a diligent public official. I'm fairly sure that Pete, had he been mayor for yet another term, would have taken two weeks off and headed for Canada to do some fishing right about now."

"There's something to be said for that," Cynthia said. "You know St. Barnabas is putting up a hay-maze back behind the church?"

"Yep. I heard about that. I think Billy's in charge."

"And Salena Mercer's going to be at Eden Books in the late afternoon to do a book signing before heading to Asheville later that evening. She has a midnight signing down there."

"The vampire book author?"

"Uh-huh. Georgia's daughter knows her agent and wrangled the appearance. Mercer's quite famous and is only doing two signings in North Carolina. I suspect there will be hundreds of fans here."

"Crazy vampire fans?"

Cynthia held both her hands aloft in a we'll-see gesture. "It is Halloween weekend, after all. I'm just saying..."

My phone dinged. I took it out and looked at the text, then bid Cynthia good luck and took what was left of my ten dollar cup of coffee (maybe $1.35 or so) across the park to St. Barnabas. According to my instant message, Gaylen Weatherall was in the parish hall reiterating her farewells and Meg indicated that I was "invited to attend" since she'd seen me sitting in the park talking to Cynthia, a well known serial belly dancer. No problem.

"Well, I'm off," Gaylen said to me as I walked in. "I was just leaving. I figure that it's about a three-day drive."

"It's been a pleasure," I said, offering her a hug. There were several folks sitting at the round table. Marilyn and Meg were there. Kimberly Walnut, of course, our Director of Christian Formation, sipping, as was her morning ritual, on a can of Red Bull. Joyce Cooper, Bev, and Elaine and Billy Hixon rounded out the company. Billy was the Junior Warden and in charge of the physical plant of St. Barnabas. Like Meg's, his term of service was up in January. He ran a landscaping company that held most of the city contracts and many of the private ones including St. Barnabas, Mountainview Cemetery, Wormy Acres, Sterling Park and the Christian Nudist camp, to name a few. Right now, he had a head full of hay straw and a nose red enough to guide Santa's sleigh.

"You might need an antihistamine," I said when I saw him.

"Dough kiddig," he replied. "Dis hay is killig be."

"Why don't you get your crew to help put the maze together?" Elaine said.

"Dey are, bud I had to go pick ub da hay," said Billy. He snorted violently. "Sebed hudred bales."

Gaylen shook her head and smiled. "I'll miss you guys."

"We'll miss you, too," said Meg sadly. The others at the table nodded their agreement.

"Well, I've got to go before I start crying." Gaylen turned on her heel and disappeared out the door. We all sat there for several minutes, none of us saying anything, the silence unbroken except for Billy's snorts and tootles. Finally he stood up.

"Bell, I'b god to ged back to work," he said. "Be hab da layout dud, bud stackig all dat hay id goig to take sub tibe."

"I can't understand a word you're saying," said Kimberly Walnut.

Billy threw his hands in the air and stomped out.

"This is our Worship Committee meeting," said Bev. "Pull up a chair."

"You tricked me," I said. "I don't go to meetings on Wednesdays."

"Or Thursdays," said Joyce, "or Fridays, or any other days probably, now that Gaylen's gone."

"We have to take the bull by the horns," said Bev. "Here's the deal. Vicar McTavish says he has his hands full with the work of planting a new church up on Grandfather Mountain. He'll be happy to celebrate the Eucharist on Sundays. But that's it. We won't see him during the week."

"That's a relief," said Kimberly Walnut. "Now, there are a couple of things I need to talk to you all about. The first is our 'Congregational Enlivener.' I found one in Raleigh who's just great and he said he'd love to come up! Only five hundred dollars!"

"Five hundred dollars?" said Elaine, aghast. "For what?"

"To enliven the congregation," Kimberly Walnut explained patiently. "You see..."

"I've really got to go," I said. "Just to be clear, *we're* in charge of the services. McTavish is just preaching and celebrating the Eucharist. No nineteenth century Scottish Psalters? No Genevan hymnals?"

"All he requires is that the old King James Version of the Bible be used exclusively. He's gotten permission from the bishop to use the 1928 prayer book. We told him we couldn't do it this week because we didn't have any."

I raised my eyebrows.

"They were stored in one of the closets of the old church. They all burned in the fire and we didn't bother to replace them," said Bev.

"Ah," I said.

"*Luckily,*" said Bev with exaggerated sarcasm, "Lord's Chapel down the road has enough of them for us to use, but they're in storage. We can pick them up next week."

"That *is* lucky," Elaine said.

"And," added Bev, "Vicar McTavish will be doing the Children's Moment. He thinks that the children might need a healthy dose of the Bible. The *real* version."

Kimberly Walnut blanched. I suppressed a grin.

"Well, what could be the harm in that?" I said.

Kimberly Walnut cleared her throat. "A-*hem.*"

Bev looked annoyed. "What?"

"About the Congregational Enlivener..." Kimberly said.

Bev's shoulders slumped. "Oh no."

"Gaylen gave me the go-ahead two months ago," said Kimberly Walnut. "I called him and he only had one date open and I had to sign the contract. He'll be here a week from Sunday."

"Gaylen gave you the go-ahead?" said Bev.

Kimberly looked at Bev with exasperation. "I asked her about it as soon as I heard about him. I have it right here in my notes." Kimberly Walnut held up her legal pad. "Gaylen said 'Not now. Maybe in a couple of months.' You were standing right there next to her. That's in my notes, too."

"*Maybe!*" said Bev, looking at her calendar. "Gaylen said 'maybe!' Not 'Go hire a 'Congregational Enlivener' for All Saints' Sunday!'"

"How was I to know we're celebrating All Saints' Sunday on November 5th?" whined Kimberly Walnut. "It's not even on my calendar. It's not like it's Easter or something. Anyway, I already ordered the Spirit Sticks."

I just shook my head and sighed. "We always do it on the closest Sunday to the 1st of November. Or on the Sunday after if All Saints' Day falls on a Wednesday."

"So what else is going on during the All Saints' Sunday service?" asked Joyce.

"The usual, I suppose," I answered. "We'll have the reading of the roll of the departed during the prayers, the All Saints' collects, and some appropriately saintly music. I'll email all the information to Marilyn for the bulletin. If you're having a Congregational Enlivener, you might want to clue in the vicar."

"I'll call him," said Bev, then paused in thought. "No, wait. I don't have his phone number."

"Don't forget," I said. "We have a short All Saints' service scheduled on Wednesday the 1st, before choir practice. I'm guessing Vicar McTavish will be presiding?"

"We're all guessing," said Bev.

Marilyn jotted all this down on her pad. "You're still doing movie night on Saturday, right?" she asked. "The 'Big Finish' to the Halloween carnival? I saw the flyer at the bookstore."

"Yep," I said. "*Nosferatu.* Five o'clock sharp. I borrowed a big screen and a projector from New Fellowship Baptist. The kids are selling popcorn and we've arranged for the Altar Guild to help clean up and get everything ready for Sunday morning."

"I'm bringing the grandkids," said Marilyn. "I'm also preparing some program notes."

"That's great! Thanks!"

"Who's going to help the vicar serve communion this Sunday?" asked Meg. "Any of the Eucharistic Ministers involved?"

"Nope," said Bev. "No one. He's doing it himself."

***

Choir practice went about as usual. Dr. Ian Burch, PhD, joined us again in the alto section and we were starting to sound pretty good. He came in early, managed to take Martha Hatteberg's chair before she got there, and relegated her to the front row. Being a charter member of the BRAs, she glared at him, but since he was still a guest, bit her lip and didn't say anything. Tiff was back from her trip and so was Sheila. They flanked Ian and both tried to be friendly, but he seemed to be only interested in speaking to one of them.

Chapter 6

The carnival was slated to begin at eleven with the costume contest, but when Meg and I arrived at ten, the kids were already pestering the folks who were running the booths to hurry up and get things rolling. Meg had business downtown, a meeting with one of her Lowcountry clients who was coming up for the weekend. I parked in my designated spot on the square—the one right in front of the police station carefully marked "Reserved for Chief Konig"—gave Meg a kiss, then got out of the old truck and surveyed the downtown activity. The door to the station opened a second later and Nancy joined me on the sidewalk.

"I heard you driving up," she said. "You might want to get that truck tuned up before winter."

"Maybe," I said, "but I think you were hearing the *Sacrificial Dance* from *The Rite of Spring*. I had the stereo on pretty loudly."

"I don't know why Meg puts up with it," Nancy said.

"Me, neither," I said. "Do we have donuts inside?"

"Is a five-pound robin fat?" answered Nancy. "Dave brought some in about a half-hour ago. We're out of coffee, though. We might have to walk over and get some."

"Come on," I said with a nod toward the Slab. "We can get a couple of to-go cups."

We walked into the café a couple of minutes later. This being Saturday, and a busy Saturday at that, there were no tables available and, judging from the line, there wouldn't be any tables available until a week from Tuesday. Someone had even taken Nancy's RESERVED sign and put it into the refrigerated pie case behind the Boston Creams. Nancy growled, but didn't say anything. Pete was nowhere to be seen, probably having his hands full in the kitchen. Cynthia, Noylene, and Pauli Girl McCollough were handling the rush with aplomb. All three were balancing coffee pots, cups, full plates, empty plates, and whatever else might be required, all the while maneuvering expertly between tables and customers in a dance that's been going on since Nooka, the first waitress, plunked a big piece of mammoth meat on the table at the Tusk and Tarpit and demanded a seashell for her trouble.

"'Morning, Hayden!" called Mattie Lou Entriken from a table against the far wall. She waved me over in her direction. "C'mere a minute, will you?"

Mattie Lou was having breakfast with Wynette Winslow and Wendy Bolling. Mattie Lou and Wynette, now both in their seventies, had grown up in St. Germaine and been best friends since they were girls in pigtails. Wendy was a newcomer, only having lived here for the last fifty years. All three had outlived their husbands and all three were matriarchs of St. Barnabas. They'd been on, and in charge of, every church committee you could think to name and if I had a question about St. Barnabas, I usually went to one of them first. Mattie Lou and Wynette could be found in the church kitchen every Wednesday morning making sandwiches for the Salvation Army in Boone. Wendy occasionally joined them, but she was now on the Altar Guild, and so looked ever-so-slightly down her nose at the two other ladies. They pretended not to notice. Mattie Lou was also the church historian and was a pack-rat when it came to St. Barnabian minutia.

Nancy went to get our coffee while I squeezed past some occupied chairs and over to the ladies' table.

"What are the 'Zombies of Easter?'" asked Mattie Lou.

"Pardon me?" I said, not at all sure I had heard correctly.

"New Fellowship Baptist has their sign out in front advertising 'The Zombies of Easter,'" said Wynette. "They have a new minister you know. He's been there about a month."

"His name's Brother Tommy or Johnny or something like that," added Mattie Lou.

"It's Donny, dear," corrected Wendy. "Brother Donny. That's what Walleena told us. Brother Donny something-or-other."

"That's right," agreed Wynette. "Brother Donny. Anyway, they're having a 'Zombies of Easter Walk' for the Halloween trick-or-treating. My grandson, Brandon, says the youth group is dressing like zombies and walking through town during the carnival handing out biblical salvation tracts. He says it's right out of the New Testament."

"So what we want to know is..." said Mattie Lou.

"What the heck are the 'Zombies of Easter?'" finished Wendy.

"Zombies, eh?" I said, mentally running through all the zombie stories I knew of in the New Testament. Not Lazarus probably. Not Corinthians. Ah!

"I suspect," I said, "that Brother Donny is referring to a specific scripture passage found in Matthew 27."

"You mean there really *are* zombies in the Bible?"

"Well, they weren't exactly zombies, *per se*," I said. "But after Jesus' resurrection, the bodies of many holy people who had died came out of their tombs and walked around Jerusalem."

"*What?*" said Mattie Lou. "Dead people walkin' around? I never heard of such a thing. They never showed us *that* story on Sunday School flannel-boards!" She pondered the prospect for a moment. "What would they be wearing? The dead people, I mean?" She didn't wait for an answer, but instead reached into her purse and pulled out a small New Testament.

"I guess they would have been in their linen grave wrappings," I said. "Unless they stopped by a shop somewhere and got some clothes."

"Grave wrappings?" said an incredulous Wendy. "Like mummies?"

Wynette shook her head. "That's not in *my* Bible."

"I'm afraid it is," I said.

"He's right," said Mattie Lou, having flipped through the thin pages to the correct passage. "Right here in Matthew. Chapter 27, verses 51 to 53. 'And behold, the curtain of the temple was torn in two, from top to bottom. And the earth shook, and the rocks were split. The tombs also were opened. And many bodies of the saints who had fallen asleep were raised, and coming out of the tombs after his resurrection they went into the holy city and appeared to many.'"

Nancy walked up and handed me a lidded paper cup of coffee. "What are you guys talking about?" she asked.

"Zombies," said Wynette. "Zombies in the Bible. I never would have believed it."

"Oh, I believe it," said Nancy. "There's a talking donkey, too. Like that one in *Shrek*."

"No such thing," exclaimed Mattie Lou, snapping her New Testament shut. "Talking donkey, indeed!"

***

The celebration of Halloween, in our part of the country, was always getting mixed reviews. We are in the Bible Belt, of course, and therefore subject to many different perspectives. There were those very conservative denominations that held that celebrating a holiday by dressing up as demons, devils, witches, goblins, and other such creatures of the night was just plain heresy and wouldn't be tolerated in any shape or form. There were those semi-conservative denominations that offered the kids an alternative to trick-or-treating by having "Fall" carnivals at their church on Halloween, inviting the children to come dressed as their favorite biblical character. Of course, when the Witch of Endor and Lucifer showed up, they were both invited home to change into something more appropriate.

Most people didn't mind Halloween. It is a fact that all kids, as well as some adults, like to dress up, and Halloween is the one day of the year that you can watch Old Man Krinklemeyer walk through the park in his red long-johns and think that maybe he decided to wear a costume this year, even though you know that he probably just forgot his overalls again.

Halloween—All Hallows' Eve—the night before the Feast of All Saints'. (This year, celebrated on the Saturday night prior due to school.) It was a holiday for kids and when we were kids we reveled in it. We carved pumpkins in the image of scary faces and lit them with a candle, not so much to frighten off the evil spirits as was the original intent, but because it was fun. We planned out costumes for weeks in advance, hung paper skeletons from the trees; then, when the sun set, ran through the neighborhoods knocking on doors and calling "trick-or-treat," all the while hoping to fill our sacks with enough candy to last us until Thanksgiving at least.

Things change.

Now parents buy the costumes at Walmart and schlep the kids around to wealthy-looking neighborhoods in their mini-vans, all the while keeping in touch by cell phone.

In St. Germaine there was still that old-fashioned feeling about the whole thing: kids running up and down Maple and Oak Streets banging on doors and shrieking with delight as some adult dressed as Barney the Dinosaur or Frankenstein or the Wicked Witch of the West answered the door with a plate full of goodies.

Moosey McCollough was a kid who loved Halloween. The other kids loved it, too, but not with the same fervor as Moosey. He was rabid.

Moosey was the youngest of the McCollough clan, a ten-year-old for whom the diagnosis of Attention Deficit Disorder might have been invented. All three of the children had been raised by their mother, Ardine, in a little, single-wide mobile home up in Coondog Holler. Ardine scratched a living making and selling quilts and working at the local Christmas tree farm. I helped the McColloughs out when Ardine let me, but she was a proud woman, lean and hard, and wouldn't take much charity. Hence, I had a closet-full of quilts, all beautifully handmade, and I suspected worth quite a bit more than what I'd given Ardine for them.

PeeDee McCollough, the children's father, was no longer around. In fact, he hadn't been around for a good long time. When he'd *been* around, he was an abusive husband. Once he became an abusive father as well, he disappeared. Sometimes, especially in these hills, things happened, and no one looked very hard or very long for PeeDee McCollough.

PeeDee named each of his three children after his favorite thing in the world next to himself, his truck, and his hunting dog: beer. The eldest boy, Bud, was now in his junior year at Davidson College. He was majoring in business and, after flying through his wine courses last summer, was now proud to be one of the seventy-five Master Sommeliers in the United States. His nose for wine was like nothing any of us had ever run into and, along with his expertise, he had a penchant for the lingo. It was not uncommon to hear Bud recommending some wine or another down at the Ginger Cat: "A tender Cabernet as plumose as a suckling calf; like the baby Jesus in velvet pants going down your gullet." And he was right. I was partners with Bud in a wine venture and when he turned twenty-one, we had plans to open a shop in St. Germaine. Bud had a girlfriend here in town, a tapeworm of a girl named Elphina. Just one name, like Madonna or Fabio. She was a self-styled Goth vampiress, embracing the coterie of teen-aged angst to its fullest, complete with the look: black spiked hair, black dresses, black boots, and a black-velvet choker on which dangled some sort of blood-vial jewelry. She wasn't the only girl in town that dressed like this, of course, but she was the most conspicuous. Well, unless she turned sideways. Her fashion choices had yet to rub off on Bud, but then, Bud was always an independent sort.

Pauli Girl McCollough, Bud's eighteen-year-old sister, was the most beautiful girl in town. She was still a senior in high school, due to a bad case of pneumonia she'd contracted in the spring that kept her out of school for more than two months. She'd managed to keep up with most of her school work, but she had a few credits to complete, and would graduate at the end of the semester. Pauli Girl walked down the street like Daisy Mae, the barefoot Dogpatch damsel, her comic book boyfriends trailing in her wake like the lovesick McGoons they were. She wouldn't have a thing to do with any of them, and vowed to shake the dust of our small town off her shoes as soon as she graduated. To that end, she'd been waitressing in St. Germaine since she was fourteen and still had the very first penny she earned.

Moosey—Moose-head Rheingold McCollough—had enough of a handicap to overcome just by virtue of the moniker given him by his drunken father after he'd slapped Ardine (after nine hours of labor) for suggesting the name "Paul," filled out the birth certificate himself, and handed it to the midwife waiting outside by her car. The name didn't bother Moosey, or anyone else in town. Nor did any of the kids make undue fun of him. In a town where there were more Tammys, Billy-Waynes, and Normettas than Mallorys, Olivias, and Heathers, a name like Moose-head Rheingold McCollough didn't raise many eyebrows. Besides, Moosey was a kid that everyone liked. His wire-rimmed glasses, seemingly always askew, framed a pair of dancing blue eyes, and although he was still missing a top cuspid, his once gap-toothed smile was almost complete and definitely contagious, even to the most fervent of curmudgeons. His head was topped with a mop of straw that hadn't yet seen a comb that could tame it. Well-worn blue jeans and coat were lovingly patched at the elbows and knees. His high-topped red Keds were his calling card.

Moosey's Halloween posse was composed of most of the elementary Sunday School class at St. Barnabas. Moosey's best friend was Bernadette. Ashley and Christopher had been in Sunday School with both of them since kindergarten. Dewey had joined them last year. Samantha, Stuart, Addie, and Lily were all a year younger, and happy to be included. Garth and Garrett Douglas, age eight, were twins and the bane of educators everywhere. All the kids were dressed in their costumes and all were gathered in front of Brother Hog's tent.

Brother Hog had erected his small tent in the southwest corner of Sterling Park across the street from Eden Books. He had a large tent as well—his revival tent—but that would have covered a good bit of the south end of the park, and the Kiwanis Club nixed that immediately. Still, Hog's "small tent" could easily hold twenty or thirty people. The front and side flaps of the white canvas pavilion had been lowered and there was no seeing inside. The banner outside of Hog's tent proclaimed "The Plague Faire," and the kids, some of whom had obviously done some advance reconnaissance, were waiting impatiently outside. When Hog finally pulled open the tent at eleven o'clock on the dot, Moosey and the gang dashed inside.

The other booths opened at eleven as well and there was no shortage of Halloween revelers in Sterling Park, mostly young, but with a good dose of parents and grandparents to fill out the mix. There was plenty for everyone to do—bobbing for apples, games, races, donkey cart rides, pumpkin carving, and candy galore. In fact, the Piggly Wiggly had run out of candy earlier in the week and people around town had to go into Boone to stock up for what was looking to be a banner trick-or-treating year.

***

It was raining like an orphaned rat's tears when we pulled up to Buxtehooters, a pipe-organ bar with all the class that the piano bars in the city forgot. The dirndl-clad beer-fräuleins were the best looking dishes this side of Blue Danube, New Jersey, and they served up the suds with gusto and sing-alongs. We could hear the patrons inside whooping it up to a bawdy three-part canon having something to do with a broom and an unfortunate couple named John and Mary who were trying to assemble it.

Pedro LaFleur was working the velvet rope when we walked up and pushed our way to the front of the line.

"C'mon in," said Pedro, unhooking the rope for us and holding back a couple of black-clad Goth waifs with one meaty paw. "Always room for the beautiful people. You guys look like you could use a Stinksteifel. We've got it on tap."

"I'll give it a try," I said. "Can you bust loose of the fashion parade? I might have a job for us."

Pedro was my right hand man, mean as a snapping turtle with a face to match. He eyed Tessie with a look that said, "Listen, toots, you may be stacked like a fat man's plate in a one-time through smorgasbord, but I like my women stringy and tough, like hard working bird-dogs, trained to the gun and loving it."

"Does it pay anything?" he snided with a sneer.

"The usual," I said.

"Yeah, I figured," he grumbled. "Great, just great." Pedro was a countertenor with a gig at the Presbyterian cathedral on the corner, but since the recession hit he'd been relegated to the eight o'clock Victorian service singing the alto line in Dudley Buck anthems, that and bouncing undesirables at Buxtehooters. It made him mean, but then, Dudley Buck would make anyone mean.

"We could shoot the works," I said. "I hear vampires have some loot."

"Vampires, eh?" He grubbed a mitt across his grizzled gills and grinned grimly. "I could afford to cash out."

"Yeah?"

"My countertenor days are numbered," he said, waving us in. "I'm losing my high Ds. Let me see what I can do. I might know a guy."

***

Meg caught up with me after her meeting and the two of us weren't long in joining the kids at the Plague Faire. Brother Hog was enrapturing the children with a demonstration of the Plagues of Egypt while D'Artagnan Fabergé was busy applying make-believe boils and flies to the faces of the children with some kind of theatrical cement. In addition, there were plenty of plastic frogs and grasshoppers to go around, and cups of red Kool-Aid over hail-shaped ice cubes. With D'Artagnan's trademark mullet a good bet to be housing head-lice, Hog didn't have all the plagues covered, but with seven out of ten, he was doing pretty well.

"Eew," said Meg, giving an involuntary shudder as Moosey sauntered up sporting a couple of inflamed abscesses with several large bluebottles sipping at the edges. He was dressed as a ragtag pirate, but now he was some sort of bubonically infected castaway that would be expiring within the next hour or two. However, as disturbing as Moosey's transformation was, it was nothing compared to the sight of Bernadette. One never expects to see a ten-year-old Barbie princess with flies crawling out of the wounds on her face. In addition, she had a bulging, dripping, droopy, rubber eyeball that she'd winked into place.

"I think I'm going to be sick," said Meg.

"Cool!" said Bernadette, obviously happy with the effect.

64

"Bernadette got all the fly-boils," said Moosey disgustedly. "She found them in the bottom of the jar. I wanted one but they were gone so I got D'Artagnan to glue a couple of regular flies around the edges." He pointed to one of his disgusting add-ons.

"There were only two of them fly-boils," argued Bernadette, "and I needed them to complete my look."

"It's a look," I agreed.

"I already had the eyeball," she said excitedly, popping it out and holding it up for us to inspect. "I got it from a costume shop in Asheville last summer. I've been saving it." She turned to Moosey. "Besides," she said, "you got the big flies. You and Dewey. All that are left are the little black ones."

Moosey grinned. "Yeah. Pretty sweet."

"Don't show your mother," said Meg to Bernadette. "She will not be able to take it."

"Excellent!" said Bernadette, rubbing her hands together with unrestrained glee. She put the rubber eyeball back over her real one and squinched it in. "Excellent!"

Dewey and Stuart ran up looking like an advertisement for a circa 1665 London getaway weekend, and not the good kind.

"Yuck," said Meg.

"Brother Hog says this is what happened when the people didn't do what God told them," said Stuart. "Also, their dogs died."

"He says we're okay," added Dewey. "We're under some kind of new condiment."

"Covenant," I said. "New Covenant."

"Yeah," said Dewey. "That's it. You want a boil? I can get you one!"

"No, thanks," I said.

***

I was enjoying the afternoon and saw Bud McCollough walking across the park in front of the puppet show. "Hey, Bud!" I called. "Hang on a second."

Bud stopped, smiled, and with a wave, headed in my direction.

65

"Home for fall break?" I asked as he approached.

"Yep. I'm having a good semester, too."

"Might you be attending the silent movie this afternoon?" I asked.

"Oh, yes. I wouldn't miss it. *Nosferatu* was voted one of the top 100 movies of all time."

"Would you mind being my projectionist?"

Bud looked nervous. "I guess. What would I have to do?"

I laughed. "You'd have to push the 'play' button on the DVD player."

He relaxed and laughed with me. "Sure. I can do that."

"Meg said she'd do it," I said, "but I'd prefer someone with a little more technical savvy. Don't tell her I said that."

"Yeah, okay. Five o'clock?"

"Come a little early and I'll show you the setup. By the way, can you give me a suggestion for a nice rosé that'll go with a pork loin?"

Bud made a face. "Really, Chief! You don't want a rosé. I mean, it's great for rinsing peanut butter off the roof of your mouth..."

I grinned. Bud was getting to be a real snob. A year ago, he would have given me a list of six rosés and the reasons why I should try them, but this is youth. I went through the same thing with music, refusing to listen to Tchaikovsky during my graduate school years chiefly due to his blatant appeal to the uninformed masses.

"If you really like a rosé with pork, let's be a bit daring and try a fruity grenache and shiraz mix instead," he said. "I'd even suggest you go with one of the Australians: a 2003 d'Arenberg d'Arry's Original. It's tart and edgy and a little bit sassy with a bouquet of cooked berries and eucalyptus. You'll taste the tangy raspberries on the tongue and strawberries popping on the finish." Bud got that faraway look in his eyes. "It's reminiscent of alpine meadows inhabited by of-age nymphs." He smacked his lips softly as if tasting it for the first time, then said, "It's about twenty bucks a bottle, but I think you'll find it's worth the price."

"Hang on," I said, scrambling in the pockets of my coat for something to write on. "I do like of-age nymphs."

"You know," he continued, "in Rabelais' 16th century treatise, *Traité théorique et Pratique sur le grandir et moissonner de la vigne*, he advocates adding sugar to the grenache grapes to increase the final alcoholic content of the wine. This is almost three centuries before Chaptal made the process acceptable. No one has even done any work on Rabelais' writings. He's totally unknown! It's amazing really!"

"Huh," I grunted, still scribbling. "If he's totally unknown, how did you find out about him?"

"Well," Bud said, "I happened to meet someone who actually had their hands on the manuscript in the archives of the Bibliothèque Nationale. Let's just say that I'm getting a lot of interesting and unpublished information. This is going to do wonders for our shop when we open it. It'll put us on the international map."

"Excellent," I said. "Keep up the good work. I'll see you a little before five."

***

At five o'clock the church was full and I was ready to begin the performance. The screen was set up in the front of the church and I had a monitor sitting on the organ console. The projector was in place and my projectionist, Bud McCollough, had his finger poised on the "play" button of the DVD machine.

Improvising to a silent film isn't easy, and I certainly wasn't as good as the old theater organists who'd play on the fly without ever having seen the film. I was prepared, though, having watched the film several times, made copious notes, practiced, and jotted down quite a bit of material to draw from. *Nosferatu: A Symphony of Horror* is a classic, a vampire celluloid that was an unauthorized adaptation of Bram Stoker's *Dracula* with names and details changed because the studio could not obtain the rights to the novel.

Marilyn, true to her word, had prepared some program notes and I'd had a chance to peruse them earlier.

"Nosferatu" comes from the Greek word nosophoros (which means "plague-carrier") that evolved into the Old Slavonic word "nosufur-atu". The name was first associated with vampirism in an article written by Emily Gerard titled "Transylvanian Superstitions" which was published in July, 1885. The article was read by Bram Stoker, and the name became popular in fictional literature as the result of Stoker using the name in his novel Dracula.

She went on to tell a little about the history of the movie including the fact that Aaron Copeland's 1922 ballet, *Grohg* (unpublished and not premiered until 1992), used *Nosferatu* as the physical model for the lead character and follows the story line pretty closely.

The audience, and in fact the whole town, was in a batty mood chiefly due to the nearly two hundred teen-aged girls wandering the park in vampire garb waiting for Salena Mercer to show up for her book signing at Eden Books. Salena Mercer had been on the best-selling list for six years straight. Her *Nimbus* series had sold millions and, since the movies had hit the big screens, her appearances were rare. That she was coming to Eden Books was thanks to Georgia Wester's daughter, an anesthesiologist in New York City, who had apparently rendered some great service to Salena Mercer's publicity agent.

According to the information that the agent provided to Nancy (as our deputized policewoman on duty) the author's flight from NYC would land in Greensboro sometime in the afternoon. The limo would then bring her to St. Germaine, stopping first for a quick, anonymous bite in Old Salem. She wasn't due at the bookstore until 6:30, but the crowd was already growing. She was on a strict schedule: Eden Books from 6:30 'til 9:00, then a seventy-mile car ride to Asheville where she'd start signing at midnight.

The lights in the nave went out, Bud pushed the button starting the DVD player, and I began the performance. There was a reason I'd been listening to Halloween music for the last two weeks. Now snippets of Saint-Saëns' *Danse Macabre* intertwined with the "March to the Scaffold" from the *Symphonie Fantastique, Night on Bald Mountain, The Sorcerer's Apprentice,* a bit of Wagner, and a little section from Bach's *Toccata in D minor.* I even managed to work in part of *Ghosts' High Noon*, a Gilbert and Sullivan classic. There was a lot of filler as well. Ninety-four minutes is a long time to improvise, but it seemed to go quickly, and before I knew it, the film was reaching its climactic scene.

Not many people know this, but until *Nosferatu*, vampires weren't adversely affected by sunlight. Like many creatures of the night, they didn't particularly care for it, but it certainly didn't do them any harm. In the original novel, Count Dracula wanders around the streets of London anytime he wants. In this version though, Count Orlok must sleep by day, as sunlight would kill him. I, of course, would greet the sunrise like any good classical musician with *Morning Mood*—music from the *Peer Gynt Suite.*

Count Orlok stares longingly from his window at the sleeping Ellen, but she's read *The Book of Vampires* and has learned his weakness. A vampire can be destroyed in only one way: a woman, pure of heart, must willingly give her blood to him, so that he loses track of time until the cock's first crowing. She opens the window to invite Orlok in, but faints. I opened the swell box and the key of e-flat minor pervaded.

I heard someone coming up the stairs to the choir loft and a moment later Nancy appeared in my periphery. She motioned to me to follow her back down. I shook my head and kept my eyes glued to the monitor. The film was almost finished.

When Ellen's husband is sent to fetch the doctor, Count Orlok enters the room. G minor, another dark key. He bends low and is so engrossed in drinking the heroine's blood, he forgets about the coming day. A rooster crows—courtesy of a Nasard stop combination and a cock-a-doodle-do motif that I'd found on page 16 of *Theater Organists' Secrets*—and our vampire disappears in a puff of smoke as Edward Grieg's familiar morning melody finally fills the air. I threw on the *nachtigal* just for good measure, and the sound of birdsong echoed through the church. The nachtigal was one of the toy stops that Baroque organs used to have in abundance. This one was comprised of two small organ pipes, mounted upside down and blowing into a water-filled pot. Ellen (obviously appreciative of the chirps echoing throughout the church) lives long enough to be embraced by her grief-stricken husband, and by the time the image of Orlok's ruined castle in the Carpathian Mountains graced the screen, I was playing *In the Hall of the Mountain King* for the final credits.

The final chords garnered rousing applause, but Nancy was already leaning over the organ console.

"You've got to get out of here and see what's going on in the park. *Quick!*"

Chapter 7

When we walked out of the church, the sun had already dropped behind the mountain ridges. Sunset, according to the weather service, was at 6:27 PM, but that doesn't take into account the peaks that surrounded St. Germaine. The sun disappears a good thirty minutes before actual sunset. We'd lose an hour when we went off Daylight Saving Time—something that would happen at 2 AM Sunday morning—and the town would start to darken at five o'clock. So at 6:30, dusk had long passed and it was almost dark. The streetlights around the square were on, of course, and although the carnival was over and the booths were closed, most of the shops were still lit, happy to offer the trick-or-treaters a handout as they came dashing by in their attempt to get to as many stores as they could before forging ahead into the nearby neighborhoods. But, it wasn't the slew of kids around the edge of the park who were commanding my attention.

At the south end of the park, in front of Eden Books, was a long black limousine surrounded by scores of vampires, or rather *hundreds* of teenaged girls adorned in what might be termed "Vampire Gothic." Blood-vial jewelry, white makeup, fangs, black outfits, and tattoos (both real and press-on) were the order of the evening. The bookstore was full since the ones inside didn't want to leave, and the overflow was starting to chatter angrily out on the sidewalk.

At the north end of the park, between the Slab Café and St. Barnabas Church, were hundreds of zombies, all walking around stiff-legged with their arms stuck out like Frankenstein's monster. They were dressed in rags, old torn clothes, hats—whatever they could find—and made up with hideous gashes, scars, and bleeding wounds of every description. Some had rubber zombie masks and gloves, but most of the costumes were handmade and scarier for it. From what we could tell, they weren't talking at all. Just grunting and slathering.

I looked at Nancy, a puzzled expression on my face.

"I caught Jeremy Calloway, of the New Fellowship Baptist kids, and asked him what was going on," she said. "You know what a flashmob is?"

I shook my head.

Nancy sniffed in consternation. "You should really keep up, Hayden. It's a large group of people that form for some pointless activity for a brief period and then disperse."

"Is that what this is?" I asked.

"Sort of," replied Nancy. "This is a zombie-walk. It's like a flashmob except everyone dresses up like zombies."

"This is normal activity?" I asked. "People do this?"

"Not old people like you," said Nancy. "Young people."

"Should we be worried?"

Nancy hesitated, narrowed her eyes, and gauged the situation. "I don't know yet," she said. "Maybe."

"Well, it's particularly appropriate for Halloween, I suppose," I said, waving to Pete Moss who'd come out of the Slab Café to see what was going on.

"Yep," she agreed. "It seems that one of the New Fellowship kids—you know, 'The Zombies of Easter'—put it on Facebook. It went viral and didn't take long for every kid in Watauga County to put on their zombie-wear and head for St. Germaine."

"How many?" I asked.

"Probably three hundred by now and more every minute. I checked the Facebook announcement. The zombie-walk was scheduled for 6:30, but they started showing up about fifteen minutes ago."

"I don't suppose that Brother Denny or Danny or whatever his name is, is taking responsibility."

"Nope. I called him. He doesn't have any salvation tracts left and he's decided to go home and not answer the door. He handed the tracts out to the NFB kids. They were supposed to go door to door behind the trick-or-treaters, give them to whoever answered, and invite them to church."

"Is anyone in charge of these zombies?"

"That's the thing about a flashmob or a zombie-walk," said Nancy. "There is no one in charge. It's performance art. They're sort of like birds, you know? Flocking behavior. They move together, but no one is leading them."

As if in response to Nancy's explanation, the mob suddenly stopped milling aimlessly and began to shamble slowly and methodically in rhythm. The vampires glared at them.

Dr. Ian Burch, PhD, appeared beside us, having just exited the church. "I enjoyed your playing," he said, "but I wish you would have included more quartal progressions utilizing the lowered 4th and 7th tones in the tertiary modal harmonizations. It might have given a more authentic Romanian feel to the 'motif of longing' that you kept reiterating whenever the heroine appeared on the screen."

"Ian," I said, "I don't even know what that means."

"Have you seen Flori Cabbage?" he asked, surveying the park. "She texted me during the movie that she had something important to tell me. I texted her back to meet me here after the movie."

"Nope," I answered.

"I think she wants tomorrow off. She's been taking quite a few days off lately. As her employer, I shall not be happy to grant her request."

"Yeah," said Nancy, her eyes glued to the park and obviously not interested in Dr. Ian Burch's musings.

"She might still be at the bookstore," Ian continued. "She enjoys those vampire stories." He shuddered. "She might not want to give up her position in the line."

"My God," said Nancy, looking at Dr. Burch and wrinkling her nose. "What's that smell?"

"That smell is garlic," said Ian without apology. He held up a string of garlic bulbs that he'd hung around his neck. "If you must know, I am quite superstitious and I have a particular thing about vampires. I do not like them. Not one bit."

Nancy's eyes widened. "You... believe in them?" she asked, taking a step back.

73

"I do," replied Ian. He pointed to the multitude of vampirey youths in front of Eden Books. "They're not all real, of course, but there are those that are, I assure you. I expect that, within that group, there are those that wouldn't mind a taste of virgin blood."

"That's why you're wearing garlic?" said Nancy. "You're a virgin?"

"Do not mock me," said Ian Burch, his nasally voice rising even higher than usual. He held some sort of wooden Renaissance instrument, cylindrical and about five inches in length, and gave it a startling honk.

"Good Lord," said Pete as he walked up. He stuck a finger in one ear and pretended to clean it out. "What the heck's going on?"

"This is a *racket*," said Ian Burch, PhD.

"It certainly is," said Nancy.

Ian ignored her. "According to ancient legend, vampires cannot abide its sound."

"Me, neither," said Nancy. "Does that make me a vampire?"

Nancy's snide comments didn't seem to bother Ian and he was happy to hold his prize aloft and continue the music lesson. "I ordered this one last week. The common name is the racket, but it's also know as the *wurstfaggot*. The sausage-bassoon."

"Unfortunate name," said Pete. "And an unfortunate sound. No wonder vampires don't like it." He pointed toward the crowd of zombies. "So what's all this about?"

"Zombie-Walk," I said. "It's a Flashbomb Facemob. Don't you know anything about today's youth?"

"Apparently not," said Pete as he gazed across the sea of undead. "I didn't even know about a wurstfaggot. By the way, how did your movie go?"

"It went well, I think. Although I missed an opportunity to bedazzle the crowd with some tertiary modal whatchamacallits."

Ian sniffed his displeasure.

"Sorry to have missed it," said Pete, "but we were swamped. Those zombies eat a lot of fries." He sniffed the air, stared at Ian for a moment, then decided to ignore the obvious question concerning his bouquet. Instead, he pointed at the horde that had suddenly turned south and was shuffling toward the other end of the park. "Where are they off to?"

"Uh-oh," said Nancy. "Looks like they're ambling toward the bookstore. *Now,* we should be worried."

***

The movie crowd had all exited the church and I expect they were rather stunned to see four hundred zombies converging on an equal number of vampires in Sterling Park. I looked for Meg, then remembered that she was staying to help the Altar Guild clean up for the service on Sunday. Still, if she missed this, she'd never forgive me. I reached out and stopped one of the small Power Rangers that was dashing by.

"You there!" I said. "Mighty Morphing Power Ranger. Would you do something for me? It's police business."

The kid, a boy I think, looked startled, but nodded.

"Go into the church and find Mrs. Konig. You know who she is?"

The Red Power Ranger nodded his affirmation.

I pointed toward the red doors of St. Barnabas. "Run inside and tell her that the chief says to come out. Can you do that?"

The Power Ranger said something unintelligible through his mask, but made a dash for the church doors.

"Shouldn't you arrest them?" asked Dr. Burch.

"They haven't done anything illegal," said Nancy, "but it might get dicey if they try to storm the bookstore. There are a bunch of bad-tempered vampires. I guess they don't like waiting their turn."

I nodded toward the south end of the park. "They're moving fairly slowly. Let's go around the square and form a thin blue line between the vampires and the zombies. I doubt they'll shuffle through a police presence. Pete, you're hereby deputized."

Meg and Bud McCollough appeared on the steps of the church.

Bud was looking at his phone, then he quickly surveyed the scene. "Oh no!" he said loudly, panic evident in his voice.

"Elphina!" He took off into the crowd of zombies without another thought and disappeared from view.

"C'mon," I said. "Let's go."

"Do I get a gun?" said Pete, following us down the sidewalk. "I'm pretty sure I need a gun."

Pirate Moosey, still adorned with boils and flies and dragging his feet just a bit—either due to his exhaustion at racing from shop to shop around the town square or the effects of the plague—spotted Meg outside the church and summoned enough energy to dash up the steps. He opened his paper sack for her to appreciate his collected booty. I saw her pull him close, take his bag, and whisper something into his ear. Then they vanished from sight as the three of us turned and set off across the park ahead of the zombies—intent on stopping their progress short of the vampires.

"Who's Elphina?" asked Nancy.

"Bud's girlfriend," I answered. "Occasional waitress at the Ginger Cat."

"Skinny girl? Wears black? Rose tattoo on her neck?"

"That's the one. Elphina is her vampire name. Her real name is Mary Edith Lumpkin."

"I can see why she prefers to be known as Elphina," said Pete. "I know her mother. Toy Lumpkin. Nasty woman."

"You dated her, didn't you?" said Nancy.

"Well, sure," said Pete absently. "She's a sexpot, there's no denying that. But one date, then the stalking began." He eyed the zombie hoard nervously. "I really need a gun."

"Sheesh," said Nancy, hiking up her belt and resigning herself to the inevitable. "I've seen this movie a hundred times and it never ends well for the highly attractive police woman."

***

Facing the zombie flashmob, Nancy, Pete and I stood shoulder to shoulder in the park directly across the street in front of Eden Books like something out of an old western. The vampires were still milling behind us, but staying in their line. They were afraid, I supposed, of giving up their place and hence the chance to have Salena Mercer sign their copy of her latest novel in the *Nimbus* series—the one, according to Pauli Girl, in which the heroine, Swanella Liberty, joins Esau's vampire clan as they face the final battle against Tendril and the coven of sexy were-rats.

The zombies had reached the gazebo and the sea of horrible faces parted as the assemblage slowly surrounded and engulfed the structure, then continued advancing methodically toward the bookstore, their hands outstretched in the customary pose of the undead, and grunts of "Uuurrrrgh" echoing across the lawn. I didn't see Bud. He'd been swallowed up by the crowd. Not literally, I hoped.

The zombie-walk moved relentlessly closer and I felt, rather than saw, the people behind us shifting in their queue. A glance over my shoulder confirmed my suspicions. The orderly autograph line had, in a moment, transformed itself into a crush of vampires. A spine-tingling howl came from the throng behind us and cut through the night. I imagined the gnashing of teeth. At least I hoped I was imagining it.

"That's it," I called out to the zombies, still twenty-five feet away. "Time to go home." This admonition had no effect whatsoever.

"I don't guess you want me to shoot one?" said Nancy.

I shook my head.

"Then I guess I'll just knock one of 'em out and see if that stops 'em."

"It won't," said Pete. "There's too many. Most of them won't even see you do it."

I heard the nasty click of a switchblade behind me and to my right.

"Shoot into the air," I told Nancy. "See if that will shake them out of it."

Nancy's Glock had just cleared the holster when the first of the church bell peals rang out across the town. Surprisingly, the zombies all stopped in their tracks and their grunting and growling suddenly ceased. The big bell rang again, a booming sound that echoed through the mountains. The zombies, almost with a single consciousness, slowly lowered their arms and turned 180 degrees to face the church. A third peal, then a fourth. The mob stood transfixed, listening to the bell reverberate in the cold October evening. Five bells, six, seven. Then, without a spoken word, or any sound at all for that matter, the zombie flashmob broke free of its collective mentality and the members began to shuffle off in all directions, save the direction of the bookstore.

We heard scuffling behind us, and when we turned to look, we saw that the aggregation of vampires had again formed itself into a reasonably peaceable autograph queue. I looked for any sign of a knife, but I might as well have been looking for a rosary.

"That was interesting," said Pete. "I don't mind telling you I was a little nervous."

"I don't think the zombies would have eaten you," I said, "but there were a few of the vampires that were spoiling for a fight. Someone would have been hurt."

"Look. Here's Meg," said Nancy. We followed her gaze across the park and saw Meg quickly making her way through the last of the disappearing zombies. "She saved the day."

Meg joined us a moment later, breathless and obviously concerned.

"What happened?" she asked. "We couldn't see. There were too many people."

"It was touch and go," said Pete. "Just the three of us against a vast hoard of flesh-eating zombies that was threatening to tear us limb from limb and use us for a reality show on the Food Network." Pete stepped forward and began to act out his part in the standoff. "I had just pushed Hayden and Nancy behind me," he continued. "'Stay back,' I said. 'I'll take care of these abominations with my bare hands.'"

Nancy laughed.

"Seriously," I said. "Ringing the church bell was genius. How'd you think of that?"

"Well, Moosey was the one who rang the bell," Meg said with a smile. "I sent him to the bell tower when you three lit out across the park."

"But how...?"

"*Night on Bald Mountain,*" explained Meg. "The Disney version. Remember? The choir sings *Ave Maria* and the church bell rings and all the ghosts and goblins disappear? I thought it was worth a try."

"Shooting into the air might have done the same thing," said Nancy.

"Maybe," I agreed. "Maybe not. It might have had the opposite effect and started a panic. I'm glad we didn't have to do it."

"Me, too," said Nancy.

Suddenly a gunshot echoed through the park, far off, but not so far as to be considered inconsequential.

"Shotgun," said Nancy, looking around. "Twenty gauge. Kid's gun." The first pop was followed by another.

"Two, three blocks away maybe," said Nancy.

"Oak Street?" I said.

"I think so," said Nancy.

"Let's go," I said. I pulled Meg close and kissed her. "You wait here."

***

It was easy to find the source of the shotgun blasts. Two blocks from the downtown square, the corner house was lit up like a Christmas display. There was a body lying face down on the porch. A zombie. Two companion zombies stood in the road, quite a distance from the door of the house, now zombies in costume only. They'd dropped their undead act in deference to their fallen comrade.

"I just called 911," said the taller of the zombies as Nancy and I ran up. "They're sending an ambulance."

Nancy ran up to the prone body. I stayed to get the story from the zombies.

79

"That crazy old lady shot Kevin," said the other zombie, the short, squatty one. He pointed toward the front door of Amelia Godshaw's house.

"Are you kids from the church?"

"Nah," said the tall one. "We're Lambda Chis from over at Appalachian State. We heard about the zombie-walk and just thought we'd scare some of the townies."

"Smart," I said.

"He'll be okay," called Nancy. "He just got shot in the butt with some rock-salt."

I turned my attention back to the zombies. A congregation of curious onlookers was gathering in the street, trick-or-treaters and adults. "So what happened?" I asked.

"We were following some little kids," Squatty said. "We saw some other zombies doing the same thing."

"They were from the church," I said.

"Yeah, that's what they said when we asked 'em," said the tall one. "They gave me some pamphlet or something. Invited me to church."

"Then what?" I asked. I heard banging and looked over to see Nancy pounding on the front door of the house.

"We were walking down the street and we saw some kids get some candy from that old lady. Then she closed the door and the lights went out."

"We knocked on the door," said Squatty. "She opens it, points a shotgun at us, and blasts Kevin when we were hightailing it down the steps."

"That's it?" I asked.

"Yeah," he said. "That's it." Tall zombie nodded his agreement.

Nancy was up on the porch talking with Amelia. Hannah and Grace huddled in the doorway. I watched Amelia disappear inside, then reappear and hand a shotgun to Nancy. Then the three women went back inside and closed the door behind them. Nancy looked down at Kevin, now beginning to squirm in pain, and shook her head. She stepped over the victim and came down the front steps toward the three of us.

"Amelia says they were inside watching a movie and they heard scratching at the windows."

I looked at the two fraternity brothers.

"The three of them were watching *Night of the Living Dead* on the SyFy channel," Nancy continued. "They heard scratching and when Hannah looks outside she sees these three idiots making faces through the glass. Scared her half to death. Then the zombies started banging on the front door."

"Their word against ours," said Squatty.

Nancy turned to the onlookers and, in the time-honored police tradition, said, "Move along, nothing to see here." Some of the onlookers decided that she was probably right and since there was going to be no police action to speak of, began to leave in order to get back to their governmentally sanctioned looting. Others, probably hopeful of another shooting, or at least an arrest, stuck around.

"I guess we can go check for footprints around the side of the house," I said to Nancy. "See if they're telling the truth."

"Okay, okay," said the tall zombie. "We tried to scare the old lady. No law against that. Especially on Halloween."

"Nope," I said. "No law against protecting yourself with a shotgun, either. In North Carolina, a person is allowed to act with deadly force to prevent an intruder from entering the home if he or she believes the intruder will kill or injure him. You were banging on the door. These women were, in all probability, in fear for their lives."

"From *zombies?*" said the tall one.

"From whoever."

"You're not going to make an arrest?" said Squatty incredulously.

"Can't see it," I said. "No jury would convict her."

Kevin had gotten to his feet and was limping painfully down the steps of the porch.

"You might as well wait for the ambulance," said Nancy. "It's on the way."

"I'm all right, I think," said Kevin. "Just stings like hell."

"I guess it does," I said.

"These hayseed cops," said Squatty, "aren't going to arrest the old lady."

Nancy bristled. I shrugged and said, "I guess we could charge all three of you with trespassing, but other than that, there's not much of a case to be made."

"I'm gonna sue that old bat," said Kevin. "I'm prelaw. I know my rights."

Nancy held up her cell phone and snapped a picture of the three students. They'd done their work well and looked absolutely awful: fake teeth, scars, detached eyeballs, flesh drooping and sloughing away from their skulls. Altogether unpleasant and terrifying. "Don't forget to get some good pictures of your butt," she said. "The jury's gonna want to see those as well as these."

The rest of the crowd dispersed and we watched as the two uninjured zombies tried to help Kevin to their car on the other side of the street. He angrily shook them off.

Nancy showed me the gun. "Twenty gauge like we thought," she said. "Half a birdshot load of salt shot through the screen door. I'm surprised it got through his jeans to his rear end."

"Scared 'em more than anything," I said. "Even so, if Amelia gets sued, it's not because she doesn't deserve it. She could have killed someone."

"Well, I have the shotgun and they're not getting it back," said Nancy. "I told all three of them that it was evidence in a possible murder attempt and that we'd be in touch concerning the indictment. I think they're all rattled enough to keep their firearms under wraps for a while."

"Well done, Lieutenant Parsky. A good night all around. Call the ambulance and cancel the run, will you?"

"Hayseed cops, eh?" said Nancy, already dialing. "I wonder if those party boys might be speeding on the way back to Boone and whether they've had anything to drink this evening or maybe have any contraband pot in their car?"

"All fair questions," I said, "and ones that only a hayseed can answer."

Chapter 8

I went back into town, filled Meg in on the excitement, and we spent the next couple of hours hanging around the square, watching the number of trick-or-treaters, as well as the line in front of Eden Books, slowly diminish. Nancy, presumably, got in her car and took the short cut toward Fraternity Row. When things were back to normal, Meg and I climbed into the old truck and made our way back home. We were greeted happily by Baxter, sitting patiently on the front porch. He nosed his way into the house as soon as Meg unlocked the front door, then skidded across the hardwood floors in his headlong dash for the kitchen.

"You think he might be hungry?" Meg laughed, as Baxter's tail disappeared from view. "That was quite an evening. How about pork chops for supper?"

"Sounds great. I'll put on some music."

"More of that spooky stuff?"

"Nope. James Taylor."

"Hmm. Very romantic. You hoping to get lucky later?"

"Why, yes," I replied. "Yes, I am." I settled into my writing chair, plopped Raymond Chandler's hat on my head, and chomped on a cigar. "I expect that my literary efforts will also have some aphrodisiacal qualities."

"Keep thinking that," said Meg. "You'll have to grill the chops. I'll fix the couscous and some vegetables. Give me about half an hour."

"I'll put them on in fifteen minutes," I said, limbering up my fingers. "The muse is about to strike."

"Who's this mug?" I asked when Pedro showed up at our table with a yegg wearing a tuxedo and a cape and preening like a CNN reporter with a fresh eyebrow wax. I snorked the last of my Stinksteifel, chased it down with a Bavarian creme-filled pretzel, then whistled for a waitress using an obscure 16th century fugue subject: a Fux reference in the third species that I knew would tickle the ear of any professional hostess in the place. It worked.

"Your beer, sirrah," said Meg. "These came this morning from your Beer-of-the-Month Club." She put a bottle of St. Ambroise Oatmeal Stout onto a coaster sitting on the desk.

"Thanks," I grunted.

"I put them in your beer fridge. Forty-seven and one half degrees Fahrenheit."

"You're the best, Doll-face," I gnarred in my Bogart voice as I watched Meg return to the kitchen. "Hustle your pins back over here and I'll show you why I've never won the Pulitzer Prize."

Meg was used to these flights of fancy and dutifully ignored me.

"This here is Lapke Baklava," said Pedro. "From Romania. He's a lawyer."

"Romanian, eh?"

"Well, we all gotta be something," said Pedro. "I myself am Gaelic."

"Gaelic? With a name like 'Pedro LaFleur'? When did this happen?"

"Last Wednesday," he said. "My life coach took care of it for me. Gaelic is all the rage and she thought it would help my self-esteem. It only cost me five hundred clams and a couple of minutes to fill out the forms."

I stared at him. "You got a lineage transplant?"

"Yep. Scottish-Gaelic," he said. "One hundred percent. Wanna see my furry sporran?"

"No."

"I wouldn't mind," said Tessie.

Our beer-fräulein, a yellow-pigtailed doll named Elsa, skipped up to the table, two sloshing buckets of suds dangling from either side of the yoke slung across her bare shoulders. She had my dinner in one hand and a pistol in the other. The heater didn't scare me. All the waitresses carried 'em. She put down the plate of grub, calmly shot a rat scurrying in the corner, and ladled

84

some beer into my stein. I stuffed a sawbuck down h
dirndl, and considered myself lucky.

Lapke blew himself a kiss. I knew the type: as dark
and greasy as a deep-fried carnival Twinkie, slimy as a
plate of three-day-old escargot, with all the morals of
an open-faced liverwurst and spray-cheese sandwich
smothered in sauerkraut--and that brought me back to
dinner.

"I don't trust him," whispered Tessie, looking up at
Lapke like he was a lawyer or something. "Although he is
cute..."

"Doesn't matter," said Pedro, tasting a bite of the
Twinkie. "We need him. He's vampire-proof."

"Wassa?" said Tessie, bravely summoning a two syllable
word, or, at least, one that might pass as such in the
world of highly paid weather girls.

"Vampires won't bite a lawyer," I explained, as I dipped
a three-inch snail in Béarnaise sauce and slurped it
down. "Professional courtesy."

The phone rang and I heard Meg answer it. She stuck her head
back into the den a second later and summoned me to the kitchen.
"It's Billy Hixon. You'd better come quick."

Two minutes later I was in the truck, our supper on indefinite
hold, driving back down the mountain into town.

***

"Fill me in," I said to Nancy. "You know something I don't?"

"I doubt it. Just what Billy told me when I got here."

It was ten o'clock, but felt like midnight, and we were standing
in back of St. Barnabas Church. I'd gotten Meg to call Nancy and
tell her and Dave to meet me. Billy was about twenty feet away
sitting on a lone hay bale and shaking his head. The rest of the
seven hundred or so bales had been stacked seven feet high in a
maze that covered most of the back garden.

"Billy said he was going through the maze about a half-hour ago. You know, cleaning up trash the kids had left, that sort of thing. He found a scarecrow toward the back in one of the dead-ends."

"Yeah," I said.

"He didn't put a scarecrow in the maze. He went to check it out. It was a body. A woman."

"Jeez," said Dave. "We went almost a year without a body."

"A new record," said Nancy with a solemn nod.

"Let's check it out," I said with a sigh. "But first call the ambulance back out here."

***

We had our flashlights out and followed Billy through twists and turns for three or four minutes.

"Hey, how's your nose?" I asked, as we turned another blind corner. "You're not sniffling as much."

"Fine, now," answered Billy. "I got something from the doc."

"Are you lost?" Nancy asked him.

"Naw. I know where she is," Billy replied. "We could have just pulled down one of the outside walls, but I didn't want to compromise the crime scene. I watch 'CSI,' you know."

"Very astute," I said.

"I don't know the quickest way in the dark, but she's in the southwest corner. We'll get there eventually."

Five full minutes (and a lot of growling by Nancy) later, we turned a corner and found ourselves looking down a dead-end passage. There, sitting up on a hay bale at the end of the hay corridor, was the body, a woman wearing black, low-cut, vampire regalia, dark stockings, and no shoes. As we came closer, more of her feminine features became evident, although we couldn't tell anything by looking at her face since her entire head was encased in a pumpkin—a big pumpkin, complete with a jack-o-lantern face drawn onto the front with paint or magic-marker. The black triangle eyes and the jagged smile danced eerily in our flashlight beams.

"Creepy," said Dave as we drew near to the body.

"How did you know it wasn't a scarecrow?" I asked Billy.

"I knew when I tried to pick her up. She's heavy for one thing. And she's really stiff."

"Killed sometime this afternoon, then," said Nancy, flitting her Maglite across the body and lifting the woman's arm in a quick rigor mortis assessment. "In this temperature, rigor would start to set in after maybe three hours. Full rigor in twelve."

"I went through the whole maze two or three times during the afternoon cleaning stuff up. She wasn't here."

"When was the last time?" I asked.

"I don't remember exactly," said Billy. "It was just before the movie started, though."

"So a little before five?"

"That sounds about right. The carnival was just finishing up."

"You have any latex gloves?" I asked Nancy.

"Of course."

Nancy was nothing if not efficient and a moment later I had donned a pair of gloves.

"Give me some light," I said. "Let's see who this is."

Billy, Nancy, and Dave held their lights steady as I took the pumpkin in both hands and lifted it up over the head of the victim. It came off with a hideous sucking sound. The stringy pulp clung to the girl's features and her short hair was matted with both pumpkin gunk and seeds. Her eyes were closed, but her mouth hung open in slack-jawed accusation. Her tongue was swollen. We looked at her without recognition for several long moments. Then Nancy finally said, "That's Flori Cabbage."

Chapter 9

The ambulance had come and gone, taking Flori Cabbage off to the morgue in Boone where Kent Murphee, the coroner, would do his thing Monday morning. He might then call me if he could hold off on the cocktails until noon or so. I made up my mind to be in his office by ten.

We looked over the crime scene for tracks, scrapes, written confessions, or anything else that might be considered a clue. Nancy checked the back of Flori Cabbage's heels, took a quick picture of the torn heels of her stockings where her feet dragged along the ground, and announced that Flori had been killed elsewhere and hauled into the maze.

"Look at her heels," she said. "All scraped up and stockings shredded. Someone dragged her in here and set her on the hay bale."

"I'll call Dr. Ian Burch, PhD," I said. "I guess he was Flori Cabbage's significant other."

"Was he?" said Dave. "I never saw them together except at the store."

"Yeah?" I said. "An assumption I suppose, now that I think about it." I turned to Nancy. "You went through her pockets?"

"Uh-huh," said Nancy. "Nothing."

"She never carried a purse that I ever saw," I said.

"She wouldn't have," said Nancy. "She was one of those gluten-free, Birkenstock, granola-girls. They don't carry purses. Maybe a fanny-pack."

"Did she have a fanny-pack?" asked Dave.

"Nope," said Nancy.

"How about a cell phone?" I asked.

Nancy shook her head.

"Ian Burch told me right before the zombie-walk started that he'd gotten a text from Flori Cabbage. She would have sent that from her phone, right?"

Nancy shrugged. "Probably, but not necessarily. She could have texted from a messenger account on any computer: MSN,

Yahoo Messenger, Skype, AIM, AOL. Or she could have used an iPad, a Blackberry, someone else's phone, a GPS device..."

"*What?*" I said.

"I know," said Dave, putting a hand on my shoulder. "It's okay, old guy."

"Well, anyway," I said, "Ian Burch got the text message. He was supposed to meet her and he may have done so. He might have been the last person to see her alive."

"You think he killed her?" asked Nancy.

"I don't think he did, but who knows?" I said. "At the very least, we need to see that message." I pulled out my cell phone and stared at it blankly. "So let's say I want to find Ian Burch's home phone number. How do I call directory assistance on this thing?"

Nancy had punched about six buttons on her own phone and was already holding it up to her ear. "Got it," she said. "I'm dialing now."

***

If Dr. Ian Burch, PhD, was terribly broken up about Flori Cabbage's untimely death, he didn't let it show. We met him outside his shop, walked him across the street to the Beer and Brew, sat him down and ordered him an iced tea. I ordered a beer —a Bell's Cherry Stout that Billy had recommended a couple of days earlier. Dave and Nancy decided to split a pizza. The Beer and Brew was the only thing in St. Germaine that stayed open past ten, even though the one waitress on duty appeared peeved. She was probably looking forward to an early night.

The Bear and Brew had begun its life as an old feed store, and when it first opened as a pizza place, still retained much of its original architecture and decoration, including irregular pine floor boards, old wooden storage bins, and tin signs advertising fertilizer, saddle-soap, cattle feed, windmills, and almost everything else the turn-of-the-century farmer might require. A couple of years ago, the old structure had burned to the ground and had been replaced by a newer restaurant, albeit still in that

Appalachian barley barn motif that was so popular in current markets. The old original signs had been replaced both with reproductions and those that could be bought locally from old-timers who weren't shy about telling the insurance company that the sign that they'd found in their tobacco barn was "almost priceless."

"Ian," I said, once we were settled at our table. "I'm glad you got rid of the garlic necklace."

"I didn't need it once the vampires had gone."

"Well, obviously," I agreed. "You still have quite an overwhelming garlic-presence, however."

Ian put his red beak into the air and sniffed, but by the look of mild consternation on his face, he either couldn't smell the residual odor hanging about his person, or didn't much care.

"Luckily, we're in a pizza parlor," said Nancy.

"Tell us about Flori Cabbage," I said.

Ian sighed deeply. "Well, I met her about a year and a half ago. I advertised in the *Democrat* for some part-time help. She was the only one who answered the ad that passed the initial screening process."

"What process was that?" I asked.

"A series of musically historical questions regarding the Burgundian school and the papacy during the Western Schism."

"Oh," I said.

"Other questions had to do with the role of the patron of medieval music, waning use of the Guidonian Hand as a compositional device, the migration of Northern-Franco musical culture, that sort of thing."

Dave and Nancy just stared.

"Anyway, Flori Cabbage was the only applicant that could manage an intelligent discourse and she was also fluent in French, German, and Italian. Some of her facts were a little off; for example, she attributed the rebuilding of the Chapel Royal to Charles the Bold, but he clearly didn't come to power until 1467."

"Clearly," I agreed. "So Flori had a degree in music history?"

"Oh, no," said Ian. "She was a paralegal before I hired her. She never went to college."

"What?" said Nancy. "She never went to college?"

Ian shook his head. "Nope. She had an eidetic memory. Photographic, if you prefer. She could recall everything she ever read. She told me she could pull it up like she was reading from the page."

"And her mistakes?" I asked.

"Probably got her information from Wikipedia," said Ian with a sniff. "She should have gone straight to the *Grove Dictionary of Music and Musicians.*"

"So you two weren't romantically involved?"

Ian Burch gave us a nervous look. "Heavens, no," he said. "I was her employer."

"Where was she from before she moved here?" Nancy asked.

"She told me that she'd moved to Boone from Charlotte. There was some unpleasantness at the law firm where she was working. She's from around here somewhere, I think, but I never knew for sure. Then, a couple years ago, she moved to St. Germaine. I hired her about six months later. That's all I know. We didn't share the details of our personal lives."

"Strictly professional," observed Dave. "That's good."

"She have any family in the area?" asked Nancy.

Dr. Ian Burch, PhD, looked irritated. "How would I know? As I indicated, it wasn't my business. Flori Cabbage did her job well. She was a model employee."

Our drinks arrived and I took a sip of the almost black brew, then made a mental note to compliment Billy on his recommendation. Ian nervously sipped his tea through a straw. Nancy and Dave were nursing their waters.

"How's that beer?" asked Dave.

"Probably an acquired taste, but I find it exceptional," I said. "Complex, sweet, tart..." I smacked my lips together, "with a distinct cherry finish."

"You've been hanging around Bud too long," said Nancy.

"Now, Ian," I said, "you got a text from Flori just before the Zombie Walk started. Remember?"

Ian Burch managed to look confused, then pretended to remember the text message.

"Yes. Yes, I did," he lied. "In the excitement, I'd totally forgotten."

"May we see the message?" asked Nancy, giving Dr. Ian Burch her sweetest smile.

"I suppose you may," said Ian, then paused for three beats. "You won't be reading any of my older texts, will you?"

"Depends," I said. "Are they from Flori Cabbage?"

Ian turned a bright shade of red. "Well, I don't recall for sure, but some of them might be. Couldn't I just show you that last text? I'd need to delete a picture first."

"I'm afraid not, Ian," I said. "She's been murdered, you see. This is a murder investigation."

Dr. Ian Burch, PhD, stiffened. "I think you'll need a warrant," he said.

"And we can get one," I said.

The waitress appeared with a deep-dish Alaskan Kodiak pizza —thick garlic crust, smoked salmon, pesto, and onions—and set it down on the table with two plates.

"This looks great," said Dave, digging in.

"Sure does," said Nancy, putting a slice onto her plate as well. She extended Ian Burch another big smile and said, "It won't do you any good to erase those messages tonight. We can get them off the server." She took a bite of her slice, chewed it, and swallowed. "Man, that's good. Once we get the warrant, we won't even need your phone. We'll have all your texts, phone messages, emails, all the websites you've visited in the last three months... it's amazing really what kind of electronic trail we all manage to leave. You want a piece of this? It's delicious!"

Ian Burch's shoulders slumped and he shook his head.

"Something you want to share?" I asked him.

Ian Burch shrugged, reached into the pocket of his long black trench coat and brought out a cheap flip-phone. He handed it across the table to Nancy. "All right," he said softly. "We were sort of seeing each other."

"Everyone figured you were," said Dave through a half-chewed bite of salmon and onions. He swallowed with a gulp and took a sip of water. "Why all the secrecy?"

"Well, it wasn't a..." he searched for the word, "traditional relationship. It was just for fun. For us, it was just physical attraction."

Dave choked on a piece of crust. Ian ignored him.

"So you lied because...?" I asked.

"Because Flori Cabbage had just been killed, of course. I didn't want you to think I had anything to do with it."

"You're a cool customer, Ian Burch," I said, taking a sip of my beer.

"Password," said Nancy. She'd opened his phone and was clicking through the screens.

"Huh?" said Ian.

"Give me your password."

"Umm... Ghizeghem. He's a medieval composer."

"Spell it," said Nancy.

Ian spelled the name, then said, "I've become interested in another woman in town, and if she knew I was, umm... had been... seeing Flori, she would be less than amenable to my upcoming coquetry."

"Huh?" said Dave.

"He's thinking about asking Tiff out on a date," I said.

"Tiff St. James?" said Dave. "Your choir singer?"

I nodded. "The very one."

"How...?" started Ian. His lips moved without making any sound. Then he managed, "How did you know?"

"That's why you came to choir, isn't it? So you could hang around her?"

"Well... yes, but I do enjoy singing."

"Save it," I said. "So you were having sex with Flori, but you were interested in Tiff how? Romantically?"

"Yes, romantically. She is the most beautiful woman I've ever seen."

Nancy had been scrolling through Ian's phone. Now she flipped it closed and dropped it into her coat pocket. "Disgusting," she growled.

"What?" I said.

"You know what 'sexting' is?" she asked me.

"I can guess."

"It wasn't just me," protested Ian Burch. "It was Flori Cabbage, too. I was just trying to keep up. You can see it for yourself! It's all right there!"

"Her last text says 'At EB in line. Meet me later. Still freaked out.' There's a picture. She's wearing the vampire outfit we found her in. Or rather, half of it. Then Ian answers it with 'At the movie. Meet after at SB. Bring the cuffs. I'm wearing garlic.' The time stamp is 5:32 PM."

"I'm wearing garlic?" said Dave.

"Bring the cuffs?" I added.

Ian's color rose.

"Well, now we know why you were wearing that garlic necklace," Nancy said.

"In some cultures, garlic is a well-known aphrodisiac," said Ian, defensively. "In medieval times, monks were prohibited from entering the monasteries if they had eaten garlic. This is because of its reputation for inflaming the passions."

"I think you're supposed to eat it," said Nancy. "Not wear it."

Ian sniffed loudly. "Well, she *was* dressed as a vampire. I was just doing my part."

"So you hadn't called it quits with Flori?" I said.

"No," said Ian. "I... uh... I hadn't called it off. But I was going to."

"She was in line an hour before the book signing event?" Nancy asked.

"She was going to meet a friend of hers and was supposed to save her a place in line. You saw the crowd."

"Yeah, I did," I said. "So you met with her after the movie?"

94

"No. She didn't show up. I went over to Eden Books and looked around for her, but I didn't see her. I came back and waited for her in front of the church for thirty minutes, then went to the shop. I thought she'd meet me there."

"What do you think she saw that freaked her out?" Nancy asked.

"I have no idea," said Dr. Ian Burch, PhD.

***

"You believe him?" asked Nancy, as we walked back across the park to the police station.

"As far as it goes," I said. "But he's not telling us everything."

"He's hiding something," said Dave. "I can always tell."

"No, you can't," said Nancy. "Ian was just showing off with that music stuff. Makes me want to slap him."

"I thought you took a class in music appreciation," I said, grinning. "You don't know about the organization of the House of Vichyssoise in 1328? Or the use of the bladderpipe as a medieval torture device?

"Blow it out your sackbut," said Nancy.

"Can you go through his whole phone?" I asked. "See what's there?"

"Yeah," said Nancy, "but I sincerely hope there aren't any naked pictures of that weasel on it. I don't think I could stand it."

Chapter 10

I was late getting back home and slept badly, having a lot on my mind, and knowing I had to be at church at ten o'clock the next morning. Still, the next morning I managed to get out of bed, finish a cup of coffee, and put on a tie before Meg informed me it was time to drive down the mountain. Nancy and Dave had agreed to go over to Flori Cabbage's apartment and look around first thing after breakfast. Police procedure dictated that we do our due diligence and there might be something to be gleaned. Besides, they were already in the habit of skipping church.

By the time I'd gotten my second cup of coffee in the parish hall and hightailed it up to the choir loft, the choir was beginning to assemble for our pre-service rehearsal.

"What can you tell us about Flori Cabbage?" said Mark Wells, never one to beat around the bush. "Ian's girlfriend."

"She's dead, for one thing," said Phil. "I heard it over at the Slab this morning."

"I know she's dead," said Mark. "That's why I asked."

"The matter is still under investigation," I said. "I can't talk about it. Besides, we have to rehearse."

"We could help, you know," said Marjorie. "Remember how we helped you solve the case of the murdered deacon last year?"

"No, I don't," I replied. I sat down on the organ bench and began to rifle through the pile of music I had stacked on the top of the console.

"Sorry I missed rehearsal on Wednesday," said Bob Solomon. "What are we singing?"

"The anthem is *O For A Closer Walk With God* by Stanford. *O Taste and See* for communion, and Psalm 34."

"I guess that Ian won't be here this morning," said Martha Hatteberg. "Maybe I can get my seat back."

As if on cue, out of the stairwell came Dr. Ian Burch, PhD. He spotted Tiff, gave her a little wave and beat Martha to her chair. The choir loft became suddenly quiet.

"Ian," said Meg after a long and awkward pause. "We're sorry for your loss."

Ian looked puzzled, then said, "Oh, you mean Flori Cabbage. Thank you. She was a good employee. She'll be difficult to replace." He turned to Tiff. "Might you be looking for part-time employment, Miss St. James?"

Tiff shot me a glance. There was a look of terror in her eyes.

"Let's go over the anthem," I said. "This is Vicar McTavish's first Sunday by himself, remember?"

"How could we forget?" mumbled Bev under her breath.

***

I played the prelude, then launched into the processional hymn precisely at eleven o'clock. The choir had gathered in the back of the church, the narthex. They'd go in two-by-two, following the crucifer into the nave and up to the chancel. Then they'd split, make the ninety degree turn, turn again a few feet later at the side aisles, and make their way back to the narthex in order to climb the stairs to the loft. The clergy, acolytes, Eucharistic Ministers, lay readers, and others involved in the service usually followed the choir in and remained up in the chancel stalls. Today, though, there would be no Eucharistic Ministers, or lay readers either, for that matter. Vicar Fearghus McTavish had made it plain that he would preside over the service by himself.

The choir members completed their trek and were filing into the loft just as I was improvising an introduction to the last stanza. I glanced down into the nave just as Benny Dawkins came into my view. He was about halfway down the aisle, leading the priest in.

Benny Dawkins was our champion thurifer, easily one of the best smokin'-joes in the history of the genre. There were those who held, with good reason, that he was the best the world had ever seen. Once Benny had won every thurifer competition and title there was to win, he retired from competition and turned pro. Now he travelled to all the major venues—Notre Dame in Paris, St.

97

Peter's in Rome, St. John the Divine in New York, and the Hagia Sophia Church in Istanbul, among many others—and exhibited his gifts with a virtuosity that made worshippers weep to see it. Many other thurifers had switched to the hypoallergenic incense due to the outcry among those in the congregation suffering with allergies, but Benny poo-pooed the practice, preferring to blend his own special mixture that was both aromatic and delightful. The smoke didn't burn anyone's eyes and, amazingly enough, created a sense of well-being, was rumored to cure headaches and caused head colds to briefly abate. Benny kept his mixture a well-guarded secret, sharing it only, rumor had it, with his protégé, nine-year-old Addie Buss. Benny had told me that the smoke of his special blend was much heavier than the smoke from regular incense and thus made it more easily manipulated. I took him at his word, as did anyone else who witnessed his thuriblific offerings. As Benny reached the crossing, his swinging and smoldering pot increased its speed until it became a blur. Addie, who was carrying the incense boat, stayed close to Benny's side, never wavering, as the thurible whizzed by her head at dizzying speed. When it finally slowed, Benny moved up the steps to cense the altar and left in his wake a life-sized depiction of Michelangelo's *Pieta*. The white smoke actually hung in the air and for a few breathtaking and reverent moments, mimicked the shimmering Carrara marble and the perfection of Michelangelo's vision. There was a gasp of appreciation from the congregation.

Vicar McTavish had taken another route in his procession to the chancel, going around Benny's artistry to the right, then stopping in front of his chair. He faced the altar, but didn't sit.

I was watching, of course, to see what Benny would come up with, managing the last verse of *A Mighty Fortress Is Our God* easily from memory. We didn't do much for Reformation Sunday here at St. Barnabas, but a musical nod toward one of our spiritual forebears, Martin Luther, wasn't out of order.

In most churches, it was the practice for the thurifer to hand the thurible to the priest for the censing of the altar. Benny had always done it, and the priest made no move to deny him the chore. I'd seen him do it dozens of times, but it was still fascinating and beautiful to watch. While Addie stood to the side, Benny circled the altar making small movements with the thurible in a counterclockwise direction (resulting in an exquisite collection of interlocking smoke rings) until he reached the west side of the altar, facing east. He then made three sets of triple swings towards east, and continued around the altar to his original position. Having finished censing the altar, and with the entire chancel now obscured by smoke, Benny retreated to his own chair, hung his thurible on its hook as the hymn ended, and remained standing for the opening sentences.

Vicar McTavish turned to face the congregation, lifted his arms to the heavens and spoke in a thundering voice:

"O God, who didst call thy servant Queen Margaret to an earthly throne that she might advance thy heavenly kingdom, and didst endue her with zeal for thy Church and charity towards thy people. Mercifully grant that we who commemorate her example may be fruitful in good works, and attain to the glorious fellowship of thy Saints; through Jesus Christ our Lord. Amen."

"Queen Margaret?" said Meg.

"Maybe it's her feast day," whispered Bev. "Or maybe she's the patron saint of St. Drinstan's parish in Old Muke."

"Old Muke?" said Sheila in a hushed tone. "What did I miss?"

"Hear what our Lord Jesus Christ saith," said Vicar McTavish. "Thou shalt love the Lord thy God with all thy heart, and with all thy soul, and with all thy mind. This is the first and greatest commandment. And the second is like unto it: Thou shalt love thy neighbor as thyself. On these two commandments hang all the Law and the Prophets."

"Oops," said Bev. "Gotta pay attention. Time to sing."

I played the *Gloria*, and the congregation and choir sang, if not lustily and with good courage as John Wesley decreed, at least energetically and only slightly behind the beat.

We finished singing and the collect of the day was read. Then, those following along in the bulletin read the direction, "The children may come to the chancel steps for the Children's

Moment." Eager parents pushed their preschool children out into the aisle, but—unlike when Gaylen Weatherall invited the children forward in loving, maternal tones and they fairly danced up the aisle to be with her—these children remained frozen in their spots, their eyes locked on the figure before them.

Towering on the top step and dressed in his long black cassock with white preaching tabs was the vicar. He growled from deep in his throat, a low growl that we could hear in the choir loft even though his mouth never opened. Then with arms extended, his hands like claws at the end of massive iron rods, he opened his mouth to speak.

"Suffer the little children to come to me," he said slowly, in a voice like ancient oak.

"The key word here," muttered Bev, "being *suffer*."

"How does he make his voice do that?" whispered Muffy. "How does he make it go all anointy and stuff? He sounds like a cross between Sean Connery and James Earl Jones."

Vicar McTavish turned and slowly walked back to his chair, and the children, mesmerized, traipsed methodically up the aisle, followed him behind the altar, and circled around him in silence. He bent from the waist until his head was at the level of their little faces, then whispered to them for three full minutes. The congregation leaned forward in their pews, and the choir in their chairs, but all we could hear was a sub-audible mumbling.

"He doesn't understand the dynamics of the Children's Moment," I whispered to Meg. "It's not for the children. It's so the adults will have some entertainment. He needs to ask them leading questions so the little tykes will give hilarious answers and we can all have a good chuckle."

"Hush!" said Meg, her eyes glued on the cluster of kids behind the altar.

His talk finished, the priest straightened and gestured for the children to leave. They dutifully obeyed, filing silently back down the aisle, through the church filled with stunned parents, older kids, and others wondering what they'd just missed, and out into the narthex where they were met by an incredulous Kimberly Walnut.

"I wonder what he said to them," whispered Rebecca. "Whatever it was, I'd like to know. I'd tell them the same thing during story time at the library."

***

The scriptures were read and it was time for the sermon. Fearghus McTavish climbed into the pulpit and looked across the congregation with unwavering severity in his ice-blue eyes.

"The Word of God says," he snarled, "that a virtuous woman is a crown to her husband: but she that maketh him ashamed is *as rottenness in his bones.*"

"What?" gasped Martha. "I *doubt* it! I've gone to twenty-seven Women's Bible Studies, and we never read *that.*"

"Her feet go down to death; her steps take hold on Hell where the screams of the undead shall pierce the sinner like a sword. Where the lamentations of the damned are without end. For their black hearts are ripped asunder and cast into the pit of everlasting fire."

"Proverbs," I said with a nod. "Can't go wrong with the Book of Proverbs."

The congregation sat, stunned, their mouths hanging open, their eyes wide, as the vicar painted them a twenty-minute vision of the fiery depths of Hell that they wouldn't soon forget, the road to which, by all accounts, would be lined with wanton women and lascivious libertines.

He narrowed his gaze and managed the smallest of self-satisfied smiles. "We are maggots and wretches, cullions and blackguards, caitiffs and poltroons, and all of us wholly dependent on the grace of the Almighty." His voice rose to a thunderclap and he pointed a finger quavering with rage across the congregation. "Confess your sins," he roared, then dropped his voice to a low growl, "and turn from your degradation."

"I confess," muttered Marjorie in terror. "I'm a poltroon."

101

The parishioners sat spellbound and silence reigned as the priest surveyed the crowd.

"God... is... not... mocked!" he finished.

***

I was playing the postlude and the choir had departed the loft in favor of coffee in the parish hall. I played the last few chords, turned off the organ and looked up to see the worried face of Ian Burch, PhD, staring at me over the console.

"Umm..." he started.

"Something to tell me?" I asked. "As police chief. I'm not taking confessions of a personal nature."

"Well... I wonder if you think that someone who might have been looking for Flori Cabbage might find those texts she was sending me. Or vice-versa. I mean, since Lieutenant Parsky had no problem, someone else could probably do it just as easily."

"Probably," I agreed. I didn't know for sure, but it sounded plausible to me.

"Flori Cabbage told me that she'd seen her old boyfriend in town yesterday morning. The one from Charlotte."

"She tell you his name?"

"No, she wouldn't tell me."

"Did she have reason to be afraid of him?"

Ian shrugged. "I don't really know, but she was acting strangely. I was thinking maybe that's why she said she was still scared yesterday afternoon." Ian put his face in his hands and mumbled through his fingers. "What if he was the one who killed her? I could be next."

"So, why didn't you tell us this last night?"

"I was scared," said Ian Burch, terror not far from his voice. "If he murdered Flori Cabbage, he wouldn't think twice about killing me as well. What if he reads those texts on her phone? What if he killed her because she knew something? He might think that she told me something and now I'm talking to the police. Can you give me protection?"

"Nope. I doubt he'll bother you. Tell you what. We'll make sure we stop by the shop every few hours for the next couple of days. At least when we're on duty. You have a burglar alarm?"

Dr. Ian Burch, PhD, shook his head.

"I'd get one."

Chapter 11

Lapke Baklava reached down, took Tessie's delicate fingers in his hand and nibbled on her knuckles in a gesture so intimate that the dead rat in the corner blushed.

"My family requires that I marry a wirgin," he smarmed oilily. "Are you a wirgin?"

"I think so," gulluped Tessie. "What's a wirgin?"

"Never mind that," said Pedro, with a stern yet resolute nod. "Lapke here tells me that the Amish Vampires are onto the Doctrine of Transubstantiation. Once they discovered that little gem, they started converting to Catholicism so fast that the Pope couldn't cook the wafers fast enough."

"What about the crosses?" I asked. "And the holy water? Aren't vampires allergic or something?"

"It's a problem," admitted Lapke, sipping his Bloody Mary. "That's why they're after the Methodists. A cross with a flame in the middle doesn't seem to affect them. And there's no holy water to worry about."

Pedro nodded gravely and solemnly, somehow retaining the air of sternness and resolutivation of his previous nod. "If they can get the Methodist bishops to approve the Doctrine of Transubstantiation at the next annual conference, the Vampire Amish will move to Methodism like Angelina Jolie into a Pillow-Lips franchise."

"Not to mention that Methodists have been garlic-free since 1998," I said. "You remember the incident at the Council of Arugula with the Cloven Tongues of Fire appetizers?"

Pedro nodded again, this time grimly and seriously, still without losing any of the gravenicity, solemnation, sternitivity, or resolutionness of his prior head-bobbings.

"Cloven Tongues of Fire appetizers," he said. "Garlic and jalapeños. Nasty business."

***

The Slab had its share of afternoon customers on Sunday, but they mostly consisted of the late church crowd, so by two o'clock, it was Meg, Pete, Cynthia, and I and the remnant of New Fellowship Baptist's Older Adult Sunday School Class who were finishing up their meals. The weekend leaf-gawkers had journeyed back to their own haunts.

Meg and I had eaten lunch at the Ginger Cat after church, but had come over to the Slab for dessert after failing to make sense out of a menu that featured Tambo-Tambong, a concoction that our waitress informed us was sort of hot Filipino fruit soup, and Gooseberry Pudding with Chantilly Cream. All of a sudden, Noylene's homemade apple pie sounded especially good. It was.

"How was church?" asked Cynthia. "This was the first one for your new priest, wasn't it?"

"It was," I said. "I thought it went well."

"*What?*" said Meg. She gave me a withering look, then turned to address Cynthia's question. "It was awful. He did a twenty-minute sermon on Hell..."

"Which was very compelling," I interrupted, "if not informative."

"Based on some obscure text from the Book of Proverbs," she continued, ignoring me. "He scared Marjorie to death. Then he did a Children's Moment that we couldn't even hear. He didn't take communion at all. He put all the leftover elements back into the tabernacle."

"That's the Reserved Sacrament," I said, taking a big bite of my apple pie.

"What's that?" asked Pete.

"During the week, the Reserved Sacrament is taken to the sick, hospitalized, and housebound so that they may receive Holy Communion as an extension of the Sunday worship."

"Not the wine," argued Meg. "The priest always finishes the wine."

"Not always," I said as I finished the last of my dessert. "There are provisions. Depends on the priest. What if he's an alcoholic? What if he has apple pie in the back?"

"Harumph!" answered Meg.

"Since he's not going to be at St. Barnabas during the week," I explained to Pete and Cynthia, "the congregation is going to have to step up and do the visiting as well as home communion. They're not used to that."

"Anyway," said Meg, "church wasn't much fun. Then, to top it all off, he didn't even show up for coffee time. It was his first Sunday. He should at least stick around to meet people."

"I sure wish I could serve beer," said Pete, looking around at the dwindling crowd. "The Bear and Brew is killing me on Sunday afternoons. Beer and football. Tough combination to beat."

"Why don't you come up with a new angle? Maybe some advertising?" said Meg.

"There's no advertising budget," said Pete. "Maybe Cynthia could belly dance in the window."

"Oh, *brother!*" said Cynthia.

"How 'bout High Tea," said Noylene as she filled our coffee cups. "You could advertise High Tea. With some strumpets and such."

"Or crumpets," I said. "Although I wouldn't mind having tea with some strumpets."

"I do like a nice, hot-buttered strumpet," agreed Pete.

The cowbell jangled against the glass of the front door and we looked over to see Nancy come in, followed closely by Dave. Nancy had her iPad in her hand. She pulled a chair up to the table and sat down next to me. Dave looked over her shoulder.

"Wait 'til you all see this," she said. "You aren't going to believe it."

The rest of the group, curious, gathered around her screen and she opened up a YouTube video.

"This is some video shot by Salena Mercer's publicist. She took it during the zombie attack on the vampires waiting outside the bookstore."

106

"It was hardly an attack," I said.

"It was an attack, all right," said Pete. "I was there."

Nancy shushed us and turned up the volume. "This was posted on Salena Mercer's website this morning. Georgia called the station and told me about it. The publicist apparently thought it was great footage."

"That's an iPad?" said Meg. "This is so cool. I am definitely getting one of those!"

The movie started, shot from the vantage point of inside the store looking out through the plate glass window, and we watched the hoard of zombies shuffle across the park right toward us. Nancy, Pete, and I strolled into the picture and set up facing the mob, our backs to the camera. Vampires milled about, sometimes looking into the store to check on the line, but mainly keeping an eye on the zombies.

"Wow," said Pete. "Is my butt that big? I've gotta go on a diet."

"I'm sure it's not, honey," said Cynthia. "Maybe the window sort of bends the reflection. You know, like a fun house mirror."

"Yeah," said Pete. "That's probably it."

The publicist had moved to the door and panned the camera down the sidewalk where the vampires were in their queue. Now we had a good view of the girls waiting in line.

"Look at the third girl," said Nancy. She paused the YouTube video, put her fingers on the screen and enlarged the image. We looked and saw a skinny girl with short, dark purple hair, multiple ear and lip piercings, black lipstick, and some sort of neck tattoo. She looked to be wearing a tight, black leather dress, six inch heels, and a necklace adorned with a silver bat.

"What about her?" I said.

"Look closely," said Dave. Nancy enlarged the picture even more, bringing the girl's face into focus.

"I know that face," said Pete. "Who...?"

"Holy smokes!" said Cynthia. "That's Collette!"

***

Collette Bowers hadn't been seen in St. Germaine for almost three years. She'd been a waitress at the Slab and engaged to Dave before their memorable breakup. Nancy might have been somewhat to blame. She'd been Dave's heartthrob from the time she had joined the force, and they'd had an ill-advised fling during his and Collette's engagement. When Collette found out, she was not amused. So "not amused" was she that she destroyed the interior of the Slab Café in a fit of pique (and by "pique," I mean "berserk rage") and almost killed her soon-to-be-ex-fiancé with a sugar shaker.

Being a joiner, and in need of a support system, she'd found a fundamentalist church willing to mentor her through her time of trial and after they'd pointed out that she was allowed, under biblical principles, to "name it" and "claim it," she'd decided to name Dave and claim him as her rightful helpmeet. It was God's plan for her and Dave to be together after all. She moved back to St. Germaine, got her old job back from Pete, and was well on her way to getting shot by an increasingly irritated Nancy when St. Barnabas caught on fire. Collette was last seen running into the burning building and, since we never found her body in the ruins of the church, we'd all assumed she'd gotten out safely and left town.

Now, there she was on Nancy's iPad, dressed in Vampire Gothic, chomping on a piece of gum, and waiting for Selena Mercer to sign her copy of *Swollen Nimbus*.

"That's quite a change," Meg said. "Christian fundamentalist to vampire. I would never have recognized her."

"I would have," snarled Nancy.

"I think she looks kind of hot," said Dave. Nancy punched him in the arm.

"Could be a cult-follower thing," said Cynthia. "Swapping one group for another. It's a personality type. I saw something about it on The Learning Channel."

"Maybe," I said. "Still, it could just be a coincidence. She could just be one of the four hundred girls that showed up to get their books signed."

"On the same day that Flori Cabbage was killed," added Nancy. "I don't know if I buy it."

"You think they have some kind of connection?" asked Meg.

"Be good to find out," I said.

"This isn't the only thing we have," said Dave. "It's been a full morning of police work."

"Right," said Nancy. "Flori Cabbage's apartment was ransacked."

"Turned upside down," said Dave. "The lock was broken. Not only broken, it was altogether missing. The door had been kicked in."

"Really?" Meg said. "Did anyone hear anything?"

"Hardly any chance of that," said Nancy. "She had a room over a garage on Pecan Drive. There's no one in that house. It's been vacant and for sale since March. Apparently Flori was getting a break on the rent for looking after the place."

"Kathleen and Bill's house?" said Pete. "I didn't know that Flori Cabbage was staying there."

"Could you tell what might be missing?" I asked.

"Looks like her laptop is gone," said Nancy. "There's an ethernet cable hooked to a modem, but no computer. There's no way of telling what else was taken. The place was a wreck."

"You guys dust for prints?"

"Not yet. I'll do it, but I kind of doubt that there will be any that we can use. There weren't any on the pumpkin. I checked that early this morning. One other thing," added Nancy. "I almost forgot. Bud's missing."

"What do you mean, 'Bud's missing?'" I said.

"Ardine called this morning. She's at her sister's house in Anderson. Bud's home for the week and he was supposed to check in every evening. He didn't and she got worried."

"Is Bud supposed to be watching Moosey?"

"Nope. Moosey's staying with..." Nancy pulled out her notebook, flipped it open, and read the name. "The Kentons, Monica and Julian. They've got a kid the same age. Bernadette."

"Yeah," I said. "I know them."

"Pauli Girl's home. I called up to the house and she answered. She hasn't seen him."

"I saw him run into the zombie crowd after the movie," I said. "He was worried about Elphina." I pointed to Nancy's iPad. "Anything else on that video?"

"I don't think so," said Nancy. "It's twelve minutes long. I'll look at it again to make sure. There were a few boys in the line, but I didn't see Bud."

Chapter 12

The four of us exited Buxtehooters to an en chamade flourish, and skipped, hand-in-hand, down the street.

"Where are we going?" asked Tessie, probably feeling like Dorothy in the Wizard of Oz, except instead of the Tin Woodsman, the Cowardly Lion, and the Scarecrow, she was accompanied by a countertenor with homicidal tendencies, a shoefly with lust in his heart, and a Romanian lawyer who kept eyeing her assets like she was liquidating under Chapter 14: Moral Bankruptcy, so not really.

"The crypt, Sweet-knees," I said. "The undercroft of St. Sanguine's in the Swale."

Lapke Baklava sniffed Tessie like a dog sniffing another more attractive dog, but slightly higher up, which was good, because I didn't want to have to shoot him right there on the sidewalk.

"I think there will be some necking wery soon," he whispered, almost to himself. "And wery wigerously."

"Keep your dirty talk to yourself," said Pedro, "or I'll smack you so hard you'll think the werewolves have come out to play."

"I am not afraid of your werewolves," Lapke snapped.

"I am," said Tessie, suddenly grabbing onto Lapke's arm like remora onto a shark, or a soon-to-be-unemployed weather girl onto a rich lawyer: same thing, really. "I'm very afraid, but I can't run away." She fluttered her eyelashes like they were hummingbird wings, or maybe bumblebee wings since many physicists maintain that bumblebees are aerodynamically incapable of flight and so, apparently, was Tessie. "You'll protect me, won't you?"

Lapke oozed some oil. "I will protect you, my wiwacious little wixen." He exuded a few more splotches, then blotted the slick from his forehead with a purple silk handkerchief. "And I shall have my rewenge," he muttered ominously and forebodingly.

Dr. Kent Murphee was a first-rate coroner and he often proved how good he was by performing autopsies one-handed. During these examinations, his other hand was generally holding a tumbler of bourbon, or, as was the case this morning, a glass of twenty-year-old tawny port. The patient rarely complained.

"Another body from St. Germaine," he said when he saw me come into the autopsy room. "Why am I not surprised?" He filled his glass from the open bottle sitting on the instrument table.

I gave him the hands-up shrug and offered a thin smile.

He put down his forceps or retractors or whatever he was using and asked, "You want a drink?"

"It's ten in the morning, Kent. Of course I want a drink. Just one, though."

"You'll love this new port I just got in." He smacked his lips in appreciation. "I like to think of it as the new breakfast food."

Kent was decked out on this Monday the same as he was every day that I'd ever seen him—old tweed jacket and matching vest, tie, and a battered pair of canvas trousers. His pipe was stuck in the breast pocket of his coat and, strangely, seemed to be lit. Under a rather unkempt shock of graying hair, he looked about ten years older than his fifty-six years, this likely due to his job, genetics, and his penchant for early morning imbibing.

"Breakfast food, eh?" I pointed to the wisp of smoke coming out of his pocket. "You know your pipe's still lit, right?"

"Oh, sure," said Kent, patting his pocket. "Don't worry about it. Tweed hardly ever bursts into flame."

"Thanks for the baby squirrels, by the way. Archimedes thanks you as well."

"No problem. It's a pleasure to order something from that company besides dissecting needles, double-prong flesh hooks, and body fluid scoops. They're starting to take me for granted."

I shuddered in spite of myself.

"Got anything on the victim?" I asked, gesturing to the body lying on the table.

Kent picked up a clipboard, scanned it quickly, then tossed it aside onto a nearby shelf. It clattered noisily on the metal surface.

"Female. Probably in her late twenties. Brown hair...."

"We know who she is, Kent. Flori Cabbage, aged twenty-eight."

"So, I was right on all three counts," said Kent smugly, taking a sip of his new favorite morning beverage.

"Yes, you were. I don't know how you do it," I said with not a little sarcasm. "However, the question remains as to the fashion of her demise. That is, assuming that it wasn't of natural causes."

Kent furrowed his brow and looked thoughtful, even serious. "There was a lot of pumpkin pulp on her head," he said. "I washed it off, but it was pumpkin, sure enough."

"Yeah. When we found her, her head was stuffed into a jack-o-lantern."

"Postmortem, I'd say," said Kent. "She was dead by then."

"How do you know?"

"If she'd been alive, the cause of death would have been asphyxiation," explained Kent. "There was no petechial hemorrhaging that I could find, and she has none of that pulp in her lungs. If she had either of those things, it would be an indicator of premortem jack-o-lantern insertion." He chewed on his lip for a moment. "Sometimes those hemorrhages are tough to spot, but I'm fairly sure she doesn't have any."

"Huh," I said. "I've seen the crime shows, but give me a refresher on petechial hemorrhages."

"Well, as you know from watching 'CSI: Miami, CSI: New York, CSI: Las Vegas, CSI: Slicklizzard, Alabama...'"

"I missed that last one," I said.

"A petechial hemorrhage can range from a tiny pinpoint red mark all the way to significant blotting that shows up in the eyes when some external means obstructs the airways." Kent took the pipe out of his pocket, put it between his lips, and puffed away. Still smoldering, it responded with a glow and a trail of white smoke.

"These hemorrhages occur," he continued, "when blood leaks from the tiny capillaries in the eyeballs, which can rupture due to increased pressure on the veins in the head. When they happen in the eyes, they're easy to spot, but they may also be found elsewhere on the skin of the head and face. Those are harder to find. The mucous membrane inside the lips, for instance, or under the eyelids, or even behind the ears."

"It's your professional and sober opinion then that she was dead when the pumpkin was stuck on her head."

"I don't know about sober," said Kent, "but yes, that's my opinion and there are many crime shows that will back me up."

"We put the time of death at around 5:30 or six on Saturday evening. That sound about right?"

Kent checked his notes. "The boys took a liver temp at the scene. She'd been dead about three hours, maybe four. What time did you find her?"

"Around 9:30."

"So you're right in the ball park. Here's something interesting." He motioned me closer to the table, pushed some of her hair aside with his fountain pen, then used the nib to point to two punctures on her neck.

"Fang marks?" I said. "How did those get there?"

"Most likely a vampire attack," said Kent, managing to keep a straight face for a moment, but then breaking into a broad grin. "Seriously, I have no idea. They were hidden in all the pulpy mess. There was some significant bleeding, but these punctures came nowhere near the jugular or the carotid. She didn't bleed out and there wasn't any foreign substance around the wounds that I could find. I'll run a tox-screen, but even if she was injected with something, many poisons are undetectable unless we know exactly what we're looking for. Obviously those aren't needle marks on her neck. Those punctures were made by something much larger, perhaps two millimeters in diameter. They're not big, mind you, but certainly bigger than a needle would make. Sort of... teeth sized."

"So what's your best guess as to cause of death? Vampire bite?"

"As strange as it seems, the official report will have to say that she died of a myocardial infarction. Certainly, there is evidence of a massive heart attack. Now something may have caused it, and if so, I do not yet, nor may ever, know what that something was, but as it stands now—heart attack."

"I don't buy it. She's only twenty-eight." I studied the body on the table. "She looks to be in good shape. She was a granolly, for heaven's sake. Probably did a lot of hiking, backpacking, that sort of thing. Sheesh! What kind of granolly has a heart attack at twenty-eight?"

"How about one that was scared to death?"

***

"I went through Ian Burch's phone," Nancy said as I walked into the station. "There was some pretty kinky stuff, but nothing that pertained to this case that I could tell. I won't even go into the pictures that were on there. There was more to Flori Cabbage than met the eye. Luckily, Ian Burch, PhD, was camera shy or I would have had to wash my eyes out with lye or something."

"I'd like to take a look," said Dave. "In the interest of our investigation. You might have missed a clue."

"In your dreams," said Nancy. "Anyway, everything's now on the phone. I downloaded his whole account from the server. Texts, voice mails, pictures, calls... everything."

"Let's keep it 'til we figure this out," I said. "I doubt he'll complain too loudly, and if he needs a cell phone, he can go get a new one. Any word from Bud?"

"Nope," said Dave. "Ardine hasn't seen him and his fall break is over. I called his dorm at the college and spoke with the Dean of Students. They're keeping an eye out for him, although he didn't show up for his first two classes this morning."

"Elphina?" I asked.

"She's not answering her cell phone," said Nancy. "I dropped by her house on the way into work and she's not there. Her mother hasn't seen her, but that's no surprise. Toy Lumpkin probably hasn't even talked to her for weeks and they live in the same house."

"Does her cell phone have a GPS?" I asked.

"Nope. I checked. It's one of those pay-as-you-go deals from Walmart."

"Bud's?"

"Same thing. He was paying for it himself, I guess. Ardine certainly isn't going to have a cell phone plan for her kids."

"So," I said, "we might presume that Elphina, aka Mary Edith Lumpkin, and Bud are together."

"We might presume that," agreed Nancy.

"So why'd they take off?" Dave asked. "That doesn't seem like something Bud would do. I don't know about Elphina."

"Hmm," I said, thoughtfully taking a donut out of the white cardboard box on the counter, a chocolate one, with Halloween sprinkles. "No, it's not like Bud at all."

"They were scared?" suggested Nancy. "One of them saw something?"

I shook my head. "I don't think so. Bud would have come and told me. No, after the movie, he ran into the crowd of zombies because he was scared for Elphina. She was, on the other hand, supposed to be at the bookstore, safely in the bosom of the rest of the dental undead."

"What's the correct term for a group of vampires, anyway?" asked Dave. "Is there a name for it?"

"Coven, maybe?" I said. "Clan?"

"I believe it's called a 'sipping of vampires,'" said Nancy. "A sipping of vampires and a necropolis of zombies."

I watched Dave write it down on a pad covered with doodles, then took a bite of my donut and wiped some sprinkles from my chin with the back of my coat sleeve. "Anyway," I said, "Elphina was out of harm's way at Eden Books."

"Unless she wasn't," said Nancy.

"Unless she wasn't."

***

I filled Dave and Nancy in on Kent Murphee's findings, but, except for the ziplock bag of freeze-dried chipmunks he'd sent home with me for Archimedes, we had nothing.

Chapter 13

St. Sanguine's in the Swale was a spookhouse of a Catholic basilica, a Gothic grotesque that looked as though it had been designed by the architectural firm of Karloff, Karloff, and Lugosi, then built by two guys with a gargoyle fetish. I'd been to mass here a couple of times. The choir was good. Very good. Almost too good for a Catholic church. It didn't register at the time, but now as we walked into the vestibule and heard the limpid sounds of Hildegard's "Missa di Stigmata," the realization hit me like a nun with a yardstick. These weren't Catholics, at least not like the Roman Catholics I knew. Where were the guitars? Where were the Jesus-fish-shaped tambourines? A Catholic church without its "icons of the faith" was as unnatural as a bald televangelist. The thought made my belly hair stand on end.

"I sense the beginnings of a plot," said Meg, after I'd read her my latest installment with artful and thespianic declamation.

"Perhaps," I said, "but not having one has certainly never stopped me before. We'll just have to see where this goes."

The night outside had turned cold and we were in for a hard freeze if the forecast could be believed. I had stacked a load of split oak by the fireplace, then built a fire, and turned my attention toward more literary pursuits. Baxter was currently enjoying the blaze, having eaten a hearty supper before plopping down on his stomach in front of the hearth. Meg was sitting on the leather couch, her feet tucked under her and her new iPad, opened to Bill Bryson's latest book, *At Home*, in one hand and a glass of wine in the other. Archimedes was in the den as well, but since Meg didn't like to give him baby squirrels in the house (he tended to leave the tails strewn on the floor), he rested, unfed, one yellow eye open, on the head of the stuffed buffalo. Earlier in the evening, I'd offered him a treat at the kitchen window, but he seemed to prefer the warmth of the house to the mousey morsel. He ignored my offering, made a beeline for the buffalo, and settled onto his spot for the evening.

The opening strains of *The Lark Ascending* came out of the surround sound speakers and all was right with the world.

"I love that," said Meg, looking up from her book. "*The Lark Ascending* by Ralph Vaughan Williams. Written in 1914, I believe. Did you know that the work was written for and dedicated to the English violinist Marie Hall, who gave the first performance with piano accompaniment?"

I looked up from my typewriter, suddenly sensing an aberration in the cosmos. "Wait just one cotton-pickin' second!" I said. "That's just too weird. Now, fess up! How're you doing it?"

Meg laughed and pointed to the CD changer. "Your new stereo is too fancy for your own good. Look," she said. "When the music begins, the title scrolls across the display. Then, just now, I looked it up on my iPad and got the tidbit about Marie Hall."

"Whew!" I said, relaxing. "That's better. The universe makes sense once more."

"But I *could* learn all that stuff," said Meg, giving me a smile over her glass of wine. "If I wanted to. Just so you know."

"Oh, I know."

"Down," said Lapke Baklava, pointing to the stone circular staircase leading to the undercroft. "We must go down into the crypt."

"Watch your head, Lapke," Tessie said urgently, yet somehow provocatively, through red, sensuous, worm-like lips, but he couldn't you know, since nobody can actually watch more than part of his nose or a little cheek if he really tries, but he appreciated her warning and did that thing that some people can do where they curl their tongues into a taco-shape in the traditional Transylvanian gesture of thanks.

"I wonder what we'll find down here?" he mewed innocently as we walked down the steps, but I knew that he already knew.

"I found Collette," announced Dave, pulling a chair up to our usual table at the Slab. Nancy and I were attacking a plate of country ham and scrambled eggs with a generous side of grits and redeye gravy. Pete was in the kitchen supervising a new short order cook named Manuel Zumaya that he'd introduced to us when we walked in. In my humble opinion, having just tasted his scrambled eggs, Manuel was a genius and Pete had better hang on to him. These eggs might be the tastiest I'd ever eaten. Noylene was walking to and fro, chatting up the customers with her usual charm, and refilling coffee cups. Cynthia was on duty as well, but she had her hands full with one particular table of demanding tourists.

Dave took a plate and spooned some eggs onto it followed by a generous helping of country ham. "She was using her middle name and staying at the Broyhill Inn in Boone," he said. "She registered under Collette Freebird, but checked out Sunday morning."

"You sure it's her?" asked Nancy.

"How many Collette Freebirds can there be?" said Dave. "These eggs are delicious! Who cooked them? Not Pete?"

"No," said Nancy. "Not Pete. Manuel."

"Well, they're great," he said. "I have the address that she gave to the desk clerk, but it might be a fake. It's in Wilkesboro."

"Did you find a phone number?" I asked.

Dave shook his head. "No phone line to the house at the address listed. If it's her, she probably just uses a cell."

"You want to go and see if you can find her?" I said. "That is, if it's her real address?"

"Sure," said Dave. "What do I tell her?"

"Tell her the truth. There's been a murder and it was one of the girls in line at the bookstore. We saw her in the video and we just wonder if she can tell us what she remembers."

"Okay," said Dave. "After breakfast. It's only fifty miles. I just hope she's still wearing that vampire outfit."

"How about Flori Cabbage's employment records in Charlotte?" I asked Nancy. "Find anything?"

"Nothing," came the reply. "Like she was never there."

"That's odd," I said. "Ian told us she was a paralegal, but maybe she had some sort of cash deal going."

Pete came out of the kitchen and plopped down in the free chair. "Okay," he said. "What have we got?"

"Eggs," I said. "Delicious eggs. You gotta hang on to that guy."

"I'll do my best," said Pete. "Manuel's wife is going to come in and do some waitressing, too. But I wasn't referring to the *huevos*, as Manuel insists on calling them, I was talking about our murder."

"*Our* murder?" said Nancy.

"Sure. I was deputized, remember? Hayden never undeputized me, so I'm still a member of the force."

Nancy frowned. "You're not even the mayor anymore, Pete. We can't trust you with confidential information."

"Sure you can. I'm the mayor's Chief of Staff. Her official paramour, if you will."

"Sounds like a great career opportunity," I said.

"It has its benefits," said Pete with a smile. "So fill me in."

"Fine," I said. "Let's get it all out there and see what's what."

"Excellent," said Pete, rubbing his hands together. "The game is afoot."

"Here's what we have," I said. "Flori Cabbage was murdered, killed sometime around 5:30 or six o'clock on Saturday night and left in the hay maze."

"During the movie," said Pete.

"It seems so," I said. "She wasn't killed in the maze. The evidence points to her being murdered elsewhere and placed in the maze."

"How about the pumpkin?" asked Pete.

"The pumpkin was stuck on her head postmortem. Perhaps to make her seem like a stuffed scarecrow to whoever might come by."

"Any chance she died of natural causes?" Pete asked.

"Yes, but we doubt it," I said. "She had two fang puncture marks in her neck, but Kent Murphee says she died of a heart attack."

"Fang marks, eh? Heart attack aside, those sort of point in a vaguely vampirey direction," said Pete.

"Vaguely," I agreed.

"Collette was in town when Flori was killed," said Dave. "She's on the video, and she's gone vampirey. We don't know if there's a connection."

"But there probably is," said Nancy.

"And if there is," Dave added, "we don't know what it is."

"Okay, what else?" I said.

"Bud and Elphina are missing," said Nancy. "They may have seen something and think someone is after them. Ian Burch is worried or says he is. Flori Cabbage told Ian that she'd seen her old boyfriend from Charlotte and that she was scared. She texted him sometime before the movie."

"She saw her old boyfriend here?" said Pete. "In town?"

"In Boone," clarified Nancy. "Earlier in the day. Close enough."

"Flori Cabbage's apartment has been trashed and her laptop computer taken," I said. "Why? We don't know, but obviously there was something on the computer that someone, probably the killer, wanted." I looked at Nancy. "I presume that nothing came from the fingerprint hunt."

"You presume correctly," said Nancy. "There were prints everywhere, and I've got them logged in, but they're Flori's and Ian's. Just what we'd expect to find."

"That's it?" I said.

Dave and Nancy looked thoughtful for a moment, then nodded.

"That's it," Nancy said.

"That's plenty," said Pete.

***

I drove out to Coondog Holler, turned into the McCulloughs' driveway and pointed the truck up to the trailer. I didn't expect to find Bud, and Moosey was staying with the Kentons, but I did think that Pauli Girl would be there and I wanted to talk to her. She heard me drive up, or maybe spied me through the window, and met me on the front porch when I walked up. The old McCollough family pickup, the one Pauli Girl used to drive into town, was in the driveway. The car that I'd bought Bud as a graduation present was nowhere in sight.

"Hi, Pauli Girl," I said, clomping up the wooden steps to the porch. "I wonder if you've seen Bud? We're all getting pretty worried."

"No, I haven't seen him," said Pauli Girl.

She had her mother's wary stance when unsure of her prerogatives. Her arms were crossed, both hands curled underneath and hidden from view. Her feet were close together and her expression was hard.

"Pauli Girl," I said with a chuckle, "you're a terrible liar. We just want to know that he and Elphina are safe."

She managed a smile. "I guess he's safe enough. They're not here."

"You'll tell your mother?"

"She knows."

"Okay, then," I said. "You need anything, you give me a call, okay?"

"I have your number."

"You can even send me a text."

Pauli Girl laughed and relaxed. "Maybe I will."

I walked back down the steps toward my truck.

"Hey, Chief?" she called.

I turned back. "Yeah?"

"Mary Edith Lumpkin. I know she's Bud's girlfriend, but I don't like her. I *really* don't like her."

"Any specific reason?"

Pauli Girl didn't answer, but gave me a sober look and disappeared back into the trailer.

***

It was late afternoon when Dave Vance's Prius pulled up to the front of the police station. Nancy and I looked out the front window and saw a face in the passenger seat. Not an unfamiliar face. Dave got out of the car. Collette didn't wait for him to walk around and open the door for her. She climbed out, stepped onto the sidewalk, and made her way up to the door in a pair of tight black pants, a black leather jacket, and motorcycle boots. She pushed open the front door and walked up to the counter. It was Collette all right, but what a transformation. Her hair, naturally brown, was a dark purple color. She'd lost at least twenty pounds since she'd left St. Germaine, then added five back in the form of facial accouterments—rings, studs, and miniature chains. She was wearing dark purple lipstick and eye shadow to match. She had a tattoo on her neck, a spider web, and another, some kind of Celtic floral design, that was plunging down the half-zippered front of her jacket.

"Afternoon, Collette," I said. "Thanks for coming over."

"Bite me," said Collette. "What do you want?"

Dave followed her into the station after locking his car. He stood behind her for a moment, shook his head in amazement, then walked around to our side of the counter.

"How about a cup of coffee?" I asked.

"I don't drink coffee," she said.

"C'mon, Collette," I said. "You didn't have to come back here. You know that. At least sit down with us and have a drink."

Collette softened a bit. "Yeah, okay. I'll talk to you." She nodded in the direction of Nancy and Dave. "Not these two, though. And I'll have a beer."

"Bear and Brew?"

"Okay," she said, and offered Dave a come-hither wink. Nancy growled.

***

"Flori was about the only friend I had here when I left," said Collette.

"What about your church family?" I asked.

"They were awful. That night of the fire, when I was waiting outside St. Barnabas praying to get Dave back, it sort of hit home. I ran into the church to find him, but I didn't see anyone. Somehow I found the back door and ended up on the back lawn by Mrs. Wingler's old house. All of a sudden, I knew Dave wasn't going to marry me, that the church had taken all my money, and there wasn't anything more for me here, so I just left." She took several swallows of her beer, finishing about half of her pint in one gulp before returning her glass to the table. "Divine revelation."

"Tell me about Flori Cabbage."

"Like I said, we were friends. We made plans to meet at the bookstore and get our books signed by Salena Mercer. Maybe even get our pictures taken."

"She didn't show up?"

"Nope," said Collette.

"Were you worried?"

"Not particularly. Flori was her own person. I figured she was going at it with that geek she had a thing for."

"Ian Burch," I said. "When did you first meet Flori?" I asked.

"Right after she moved to town, I think. Maybe four years ago. She lived in Boone when I was here. She'd just moved from Charlotte and was looking for a job. She came into the Slab one day and we just hit it off."

"Did you know anything about a boyfriend?"

"Here? In St. Germaine? Ian?"

"No," I said. "In Charlotte. It seems she had a boyfriend. Maybe someone she was afraid of?"

"She never mentioned a boyfriend."

"How about family? We haven't been able to find any family."

Collette shook her head. "She told me she didn't have any. I took her down to Spartanburg a couple of times for Thanksgiving with my folks."

"Do you know where she worked? In Charlotte, I mean. We've looked but can't find any record of her employment."

"She worked as a paralegal, but she didn't have a permanent position. She worked as an independent contractor."

"Aw, nuts," I said. "Another dead end."

"She did tell me that she worked for one law firm for about a year. As a contractor."

I looked at Collette. This was a different girl than the one who had left St. Germaine three years ago, and it wasn't just the physical transformation. She was tougher, more self-assured.

"Something with ABBA in the title. I remember because we laughed about it."

I looked at her, puzzled.

"You know," she said, "ABBA. The singing group? 'Dancing Queen?'"

"I'll check it out," I said. "You going to stick around?"

"Nah. Dave said he'd drive me home."

I stuck out my hand. "It's good to see you, Collette. Thanks for your help."

She took it.

Chapter 14

We snuck into the crypt and looked around at ten empty caskets.

"Where do you think they are?" asked Pedro. "Taking a coffin break?"

"That line's been done to undeath," I said. "They're here. I can smell 'em."

"Oh, they are here all right," said Lapke Baklava with a swirl of his cape. "And now we've got you, too."

"Lucky I slipped into my garlic-flavored pantaloons," said Pedro with a determined grin. "You have yours on?"

"Not me," I said. "I have a date later."

***

It didn't take long to find a law firm in Charlotte that included only the initials A and B. Aaron, Brokovitz and Adger, Attorneys at Law. Seven years ago, the initials were ABBA, but the firm had dropped one of the partners when he plead guilty to manslaughter and was sent up the river for fifteen years. That partner's name was Brannon. Rob Brannon.

Carol Sterling introduced me to him four years ago when he moved to town. "Rob's been a visitor here at St. Barnabas since he was born," she said. "His family's from St. Germaine, but he's never really lived here."

When the old church stood, it was easy enough to find the Brannon name amongst the good and great. Rob's ancestors were among the founding members of St. Barnabas and there were three earlier Robert Brannons memorialized in the stained glass windows. This Rob Brannon though, Rob Brannon, IV, was a different story. He'd tried to legally lay claim to thirty-four million dollars that St. Barnabas Church had in an old account, but had no idea that it was still entitled to. When the church treasurer, Randall Stamps, got in the way of the deal, Rob arranged for his untimely death. It was a closed case and we'd put the rascal away, although the church still bore some of the divisive scars that he'd inflicted. That Flori Cabbage had worked for Brannon in Charlotte was no coincidence.

"Find out where he's doing his time, and schedule us an appointment with him," I told Nancy. "I've got a meeting over at the church. I'll be back in about thirty minutes."

"Don't your meetings take four or five hours?" asked Nancy with a snarky smile.

"Half an hour," I growled. "Maybe sooner. Dave come in this morning yet?"

"Nope."

***

"Today is All Saints' Day, November 1st," sniffed Bev. "We're celebrating it this Sunday. It's one month 'til Advent starts. We ought to have at least one staff meeting before Christmas, don't you think?"

"You guys can have as many meetings as you like," I said, pouring myself a cup of coffee from the carafe that Marilyn had thoughtfully put on the table. "In fact, I affirm your meetings."

"Can you tell us anything about poor Flori Cabbage?" asked Joyce Cooper.

I shook my head. "I really can't. I will tell you, for what it's worth, that we think she was killed elsewhere and then dragged into the hay maze."

"Terrible thing," said Joyce.

"Speaking of terrible," said Kimberly Walnut, "do you know when Vicar McTavish is coming in? I needed to ask him something about Sunday's service, but I can never seem to catch him."

Bev shook her head. "Vicar McTavish is only here on Sundays. He's working up on Grandfather Mountain."

"Oh, *brother!*" said Kimberly. "By the way, can we get Clarence to clean the children's bathroom upstairs once in a while? It's like a pig sty up there! You'd think that a janitor would know his job!"

"Sexton," Bev said with a weary sigh. "Clarence is a sexton."

"What was it the vicar said to the kids during the Children's Moment last Sunday?" asked Joyce. "I've never seen them so quiet."

"They wouldn't tell me," huffed Kimberly Walnut. "The only information I could wheedle out of one of them was that the Father said that they mustn't ever tell what he told them. It was a secret and did they know what a secret was?"

"Apparently, they do," I said with a smile.

"I asked one of the parents, but they couldn't get anything, either. And here's something else..."

"I've got to get back to work," I interrupted. "Anything I should know about the service on Sunday?"

"Just the normal 1928 All Saints' liturgy with a throwback, 19th century Scottish Calvinist priest," said Bev. "Should be interesting. What are we singing?"

"We're doing the Puccini *Requiem*."

"The whole thing?" asked Joyce.

"It's not a requiem mass. Just an anthem, but very nice. We'll do it during the offertory."

"The bulletin's almost finished," said Marilyn. "It's in the office if anyone wants to see it. I'm still waiting for the list of the dearly departed." She looked at me, then smiled and said, "Hayden's already sent his stuff in."

"Don't forget that we have the Congregational Enlivener here on Sunday," said Kimberly Walnut. "He'll be meeting with the Sunday School classes and telling us why our church is so... well... boring. Then we'll be handing out the Spirit Sticks for the kids to use during the service. The vestry is all on board."

"Has your Congregational Enlivener actually been to one of our services?" I asked.

"No," said Kimberly Walnut, "but I told him how boring they are. Up, down, up, down, sing this old hymn, sing that boring Psalm, read the scripture, recite some old creed... It's the same thing every Sunday. I tried to clear all this with Vicar McTavish..."

Bev bit her lip. "Kimberly, I'd like to see you after the meeting," she said sweetly.

Kimberly Walnut didn't take the hint. "Anyway," she continued, "our Enlivener will be interjecting some fun elements into the service. We've decided that they should be a surprise."

"This should work well, what with us using the '28 Prayer Book and everything," I said as I stood to leave. "The vicar will love it."

"Now, about Advent," continued Kimberly Walnut. "There are several of us that think St. Barnabas should really do away with it entirely. A lot of churches are doing just that, you know. If we had Christmas carols for the whole month of December instead of those gloomy Advent hymns, it'd put everyone in a great holiday mood!"

I made for the door. "I'll see you guys later."

Bev caught up to me just down the hall. "She's got to go!" she hissed. "But I can't fire her! The vestry voted that there will be no personnel changes until we get a permanent rector. She knows it and has been biding her time. Not only that, but now she has a couple of vocal supporters."

"Then I guess we'd better enliven them," I said. "What's the worst that can happen?"

***

"Guess what?" said Nancy as I entered the station.

"I can't imagine," I said. "Where the heck is Dave?"

"Where do you think?" said Nancy.

"Well, he's not at home," I said. "I drove by his place on the way in. His car is gone."

"Right," said Nancy with a sarcastic roll of her eyes. "And you call yourself a detective."

"Oh," I said. "Wilkesboro."

"He called and said he'd be here by lunch. Meanwhile, there's other news. I called the Avery-Mitchell Correctional Institution in Spruce Pine to schedule an interview with Robert Brannon."

"Yeah?"

"I couldn't get one. Know why?"

"He's out, isn't he?" I said.

"Yep. Paroled last month. He did four years of a fifteen year sentence. They're out of space, Rob was a model prisoner, and manslaughter was a lesser offense, so he was paroled out of there."

"Did you call his parole officer?"

"I did," said Nancy. "Brannon checked in the first week, but the parole officer hasn't heard from him since then. The guy is so busy that he hasn't even scheduled any appointments with Rob yet."

"Oh, *great*. Does he have Rob Brannon's address? A phone number?"

"Got the address," said Nancy. "It's an apartment in Newland. I talked to the manager. Brannon paid three months in advance. The manager hasn't seen him for a couple of weeks. There's a phone number, too, but no answer. I'll send Dave up there to check it out, but I'm betting he's not there."

I tapped absently on the desk, my mind racing.

"Well, that explains Flori Cabbage spotting her old boyfriend," I said. "But what's he doing in Watauga County?"

"Remember at his sentencing hearing?" said Nancy. "He said he'd get even with St. Barnabas. Not just you. The whole church."

I nodded. "Let's say he did have something to do with murdering Flori Cabbage. Why? Why after four years?"

"It can't be coincidence," said Nancy, shaking her head. "I just don't know."

"I need a Reuben sandwich," I said. "Sauerkraut always helps me think."

***

Seventeen minutes later, Noylene Fabergé-Dupont-McTavish was setting a plate down in front of me. On this plate rested the champion sandwich of all time, the Reuben. Winner of the 1956 International Sandwich Exposition, it purportedly had a much longer history, having been simultaneously invented in 1914 by Arnold Reuben, owner of Reuben's Restaurant and Delicatessen in New York, by Reuben Kulakofsky, a wholesale grocer in Omaha, Nebraska, and by William Hamerly, a New York accountant and bachelor cook, who named it after Arnold Reuben. Whoever it was that came up with the recipe—corned beef, sauerkraut, Swiss cheese, and Thousand Island dressing on rye bread—was a bona fide American hero in my book and should have his own holiday, a plot in the Arlington cemetery, and possibly have his likeness (or one of the sandwich) issued on a postage stamp. Certainly, U.S. Postal Service and other government employees around the country would embrace this idea. What was one more holiday?

"You sure you don't want anything?" Noylene asked Nancy.

"Maybe just some onion rings," said Nancy, now that the scent of deep-fried breaded onions was wafting from my plate. "Onion rings and a sweet tea."

Brother Hog was sitting at the counter, bouncing little Rahab on his knee and digging into a plate of meatloaf and mashed potatoes.

"Afternoon, Brother Hog," I said. "Your brother is quite a preacher. Must run in the family."

"Fearghus? Yes, I suppose he is, although he embraces a different interpretation of the scriptures than I do. Still, it takes all kinds to get through to people, doesn't it?"

"I suppose it does," I said, tickling Rahab under his chubby chin. "How's that little nipper doing today?"

"Doing great," said Hog. "He'll be a year old in a month or so. You know, I wonder if he might be walking by now if we hadn't snipped off his tail when he was circumcised."

"Good point," I said. "Although little Rahab will probably be glad you did when he gets to kindergarten. There're not too many kids walking around with tails these days. You know, I've read that baby kangaroos use their tails to learn how to walk. I think that's true of many caudated bipeds."

"Interesting," said Brother Hog, with a bob of his head. Noylene, overhearing, rolled her eyes.

"Is he preaching yet?" asked Nancy. "I read about this little baby preacher in Iowa. Right now he's just preaching to the family pigs, but they seem to be quite amenable to the Gospel. In a year or so his daddy's going to take him on the circuit."

"Little Rahab's not ready just yet," said Brother Hog. "Won't be long, though. He's already been rebuking the unclean spirit of diaper rash."

Chapter 15

Ten little bats fluttered down into the coffins and transmogrified into the Vampire Amish with little poofs of smoke, sort of like a leaf-blower with some bad gas, the same leaf-blower you told yourself you'd empty out before putting it away last October but never did so the gas went bad, like that, but not as loud. I looked at Tessie just in time to see her expensively capped fangs extend over her meager but lovely TV lips.

"Vampires," said Pedro with a shrug, then turned his attention to Tessie. "I suppose your sister isn't even in trouble?"

"Not only that," chuckled Tessie. "I don't even have a sister."

"What do you want with us, then?" I said.

"You have certain skills we need," said Lapke. He looked at me like the vampire rat that had all the Blut-Käse and knew just how to eat it. "You probably don't recognize me, since you thought I was dead."

His accent disappeared and suddenly, everything became as clear as a very clean windshield right after it's been cleaned by one of those guys waiting at the stoplight that you really don't want to clean your windshield, but he does it anyway and then you slide a dollar out of the top of your window out of guilt and he cusses you for the cheap skinflint that you are, but you didn't want him to clean it in the first place and who asked him and why doesn't he get a real job so you drive away with a clear conscience, just as clear as your windshield.

It was Race. Father Race Rankle. I had watched him die, or thought I had, in my office, poisoned by Lilith Hammerschmidt after Race had squelched her dream of being the upstairs maid at a high-rise leper colony that was permanently unclean.

"Oh, I was dead all right," said Father Rankle, obviously reading my thought-bubble narrative. "Undead to be exact."

***

Our short All Saints' service was uneventful. Vicar McTavish had declined to preside, having pressing business at Grandfather Mountain, so we made do with a couple of hymns, scripture readings, and prayers. When we were finished, the choir members who were present (and who comprised most of the congregation) dutifully made their way up the steps to the choir loft.

"Better and better," said Muffy LeMieux, perusing my latest chapter. "I think you've really got something going here. I just love the Amish vampires. I can just picture them in their little outfits with their little hats and beards. They're so cute!"

"Don't encourage him," said Meg. "A man that flattereth his neighbor spreadeth a net for his feet."

"Huh?" I said.

Meg held her iPad up. "Proverbs 29:5-6. 'In the transgression of a bad writer there is a snare: but the righteous one doth sing and rejoice.'"

"Methinks you may be editorializing," I said.

"Well, I really hate vampires."

"Here's my favorite proverb," said Mark Wells. "'Do not eat anything you find already dead. You may give it to an alien.'"

"*What?*" exclaimed Tiff. "Why would anyone eat anything they found already dead?" She'd vacated her usual seat and moved forward a row to sit next to Martha in anticipation of Dr. Ian Burch's arrival. All the altos had.

"Who are these aliens you speak of?" asked Randy from the tenor section. "I thought the Bible says that there aren't any aliens."

I sighed.

"What about Jonah?" said Rebecca. "Remember when Hayden proved that Jonah was in the belly of a spaceship for three days? Those were probably aliens. Or else ancient Egyptians with spaceships."

"I did no such thing," I said. "Now let's look at the Puccini *Requiem*. We'll plan to sing it at the offertory, but I don't really

134

know what's going to happen on Sunday, because Kimberly Walnut has a Congregational Enlivener coming to the service."

"I heard about that," said Sheila. "Is it true they're passing out Spirit Sticks?"

"To the kids," Bev said. "Just to the kids."

"What do you do with a Spirit Stick?" asked Steve. "Isn't that some sort of pep-rally thing?"

"A pep-rally for Jesus," said Bev with a heavy sigh. "That's just great."

"I saw the sticks," said Elaine. "They were in the office. The box said they were 'Boomwhackers,' whatever those are."

"Yes," I said. "I hate to interrupt, but we should really look at this anthem..."

"I know what Boomwhackers are," said Tiff. "We have to use them in our elementary ed music classes. They're plastic tubes you bang on things or hit with mallets. They make sort of a hollow sound, but they're tuned to the musical scale."

"Better and better," said Bev.

"You see," I continued, "Mr. Puccini didn't write an entire requiem, he just..."

"HONNNNK!" went Dr. Ian Burch's nose as it announced his arrival, followed by a nasal, "Sorry I'm late. Has anyone seen Tiff?" He spotted her a second later, frowned, and glared at Martha as if the new seating arrangements were her fault. "What's going on here?" he sputtered.

"Hi, Ian," I said. "We were just getting started. I put Tiff up here in with Martha in the front row because I thought the blend would be better."

"It certainly will not!" said Ian emphatically. "In point of fact, in a monograph by François de Baptiste in 1456..."

"That's an excellent point!" I said. "So after the introduction, everyone is in unison at measure six..."

"You know what I heard?" said Phil. "I heard that we were having that crazy civet cat coffee for coffee hour after the service on Sunday. Kimmy Jo Jameson donated it for the All Saints' Day celebration. It's like twenty bucks a cup!"

"Where did you hear that?" Bob Solomon asked.

"Mattie Lou Entriken told me. She and Wynette had to sign for it. We're also having coffee cakes, tortes, cannolis... the works! All courtesy of Yardborough's bakery."

"You know who liked coffee," said Ian Burch, sadly and almost to himself. "Flori Cabbage. Flori Cabbage liked coffee."

"I've seen it advertised over at Holy Grounds," said Rebecca. "Kylie Moffit says it's the world's finest coffee, but I never bought any. It's way too expensive. I'd certainly try it."

"I don't even like coffee," said Sheila, "and I'm going to try it."

"I had a taste once," said Muffy. "It's called Kopi Luwak. The cat eats the beans and poops 'em back out. It was good I guess, but I kept thinking I tasted a little litter-box flavor."

"I'm sure we'll all be happy to give it a try," I said. "Now then, following along, at measure twenty-nine..."

"Here it is!" Marjorie sang out, waving a pew Bible aloft. "Proverbs 31:6. 'Give beer to those who are perishing, wine to those who are in anguish.'"

"What are you talking about?" said Dr. Ian Burch, PhD.

"Try to keep up, Ian," said Marjorie patiently. "We're discussing the Proverbs. I think it's fair to say that this is a scripture that can speak to all of us. Now, let us pray..."

***

Thursday morning dawned cold and gray. I had a feeling leaf season was over. There were still a few colors left on the trees to be sure, but when the forecasted weather front came over the mountains, it was only a matter of days before the rain would beat the remaining foliage into soggy submission. It was one of those mornings when running was going to be a chore, and although I'd been diligent over the past few weeks, I was now thinking seriously about buying a treadmill. Still, Baxter enjoyed the run and as long as it wasn't raining buckets, I decided that the two mile jog down the road and back was worth the effort. Two miles for me, about sixteen for Baxter by the time he'd finished with every squirrel, groundhog, and rabbit within sniffing distance.

I got back to the house just as the drizzle started. Baxter decided that a little rain never bothered a dog of his stature and took off to the river after a family of beavers that had been taunting him since July. I walked into the kitchen and kissed Meg on top of her head. She was sitting at the kitchen table drinking a cup of Earl Grey tea, her particular favorite, and reading the latest issue of *Harper's* magazine.

"Good morning," I said. "Coffee?"

"Already made. Have any revelations while you were running?"

"Yep. I did." I got the coffee pot and poured myself a mugful, and sat down opposite Meg. She was beautiful in the morning. She was beautiful anytime, but in her robe, with her black hair tousled and her face scrubbed, she took my breath away.

"Well?" She closed her magazine, picked up her tea with both hands, and blew across the cup. Her gray eyes danced across the table top and she accorded me her full attention.

"Here's the thing," I said. "Where'd he get the pumpkin?"

A look of confusion crossed her face. "Where'd who get what pumpkin?"

"Where did the guy who killed Flori Cabbage get the pumpkin that he stuck on her head after he killed her? There weren't any pumpkins in the hay maze. There weren't any pumpkins available in town at all. Roger at the Pig never ordered any. The only place he could have gotten one..."

"Was at the carnival," said Meg. "Of course! The DaNGLs were selling pumpkins. They were doing pumpkin carving at their booth."

"Right. But this pumpkin wasn't carved. He didn't have time to carve it, or maybe didn't want her face seen through the gaps. He just drew a face on it with magic marker."

"Then cut the bottom out and stuck it on her head," said Meg.

"So if Flori Cabbage was killed between 5:30 and six, or there about, the carnival would have been shutting down. The pumpkin was probably an afterthought, meant to confuse anyone who found

137

her into thinking she was part of the spooky decor. Maybe give the killer a couple of hours head start. Maybe give him time to search her house."

"The carnival was closing up," said Meg, "so whoever it was that got it was probably the last person at the booth. I mean, who would buy a pumpkin at the end of a Halloween celebration?"

"Exactly."

"One of the DaNGLs might remember who that was," said Meg.

"Maybe," I said. "But I sure don't want to go out to Camp Possumtickle."

"Camp Daystar," Meg corrected.

"Yeah. Wanna come with me?"

"No, thank you!"

***

The clouds had come in low and they hung in the hollers of the mountains like the smoke that gave the range its name. I drove my old truck carefully around the curves, the fog appearing and disappearing depending on the bend in the road. The rain was still spitting and my wipers were clicking almost in time with the recording of Beethoven's Second that I had in the CD player. The leaves would start dropping in bushel baskets as soon as the rain started in earnest. The merchants in the region had all been hoping for one more good weekend, but it wasn't to be. The next influx of visitors into our little town would be Thanksgiving weekend and would continue through Christmas.

A flock of wild turkeys, eight or nine in all, skipped across the road in front of me and I tapped on the brakes to slow my speed. A car passed me in the opposite direction and I flashed my headlights, a signal for the driver to turn on his own. I checked my rear-view mirror. He did. Beethoven's symphony went into the second movement, one of my favorites. Ten minutes long, it is one of Beethoven's most enjoyable symphonic slow movements and perfect for driving in the mountains. I'd have to treat Meg to this one, I decided.

I pulled into the town square just as the double-reed quartet was beginning their side-slapping Austrian *scherzo* in the third movement. Nancy was standing in the road outside the station leaning into a car window. I pulled into my parking spot and got out of the car just as she finished up, waved at the driver, and hustled into the station out of the nasty weather.

"What a miserable day," she said. "That guy was lost. He was looking for Banner Elk."

"I'll bet he's glad he found you, then. Most folks would have sent him straight to 184. I'll bet you pointed him toward that shortcut up Old Chambers."

Nancy grinned. "Maybe."

"I had a thought this morning," I said, then filled her in on my pumpkin theory.

"Sheesh," said Nancy. "Why didn't I think of that?"

"Well, I am the chief," I said modestly. "It's my job to be brilliant and astute with occasional flashes of... umm... astute brilliance."

"Yes," said Nancy. "Yes, it is. Are you going out to the camp?"

"Guess I have to. And you're coming along with me."

"Me? You don't need me tagging along. Take Dave. He'll be in at ten."

"Nope. *You,* Lieutenant Parsky."

Chapter 16

"I've swum the Tiber," said Race. "I've donned the Shroud of St. Helmuth and become a mackerel-snapper. Now we're taking back St. Sanguine's from these Latin-chanting, incense-smoking, confession-saying, saint-praying snootyboots that have had it their own way for too long."

"Too long being 'bout two-thousand years," muttered Pedro.

"We need a couple guys that can find out stuff," said Race. "And a cantor. You can't refuse if you're one of us!"

I tugged nervously at my collar. Pedro adjusted his pantaloons.

"Besides," Race continued, pointing a bony, litigious finger up towards the chapel, "these guys are dinosaurs. No one chants anymore and no one will miss them. We're going to be the latest word in denominations. Think of all those vampire-reading teenagers whose parents want them to go back to church."

"I don't see it, Race," I said. "Look around. How are you going to do it? What about services? These Amish have no musical tradition at all. Maybe one or two of them can manage an autoharp..."

Race shook his head with a dry rattle. "It's not about them. They're just our minions. We're moving the Vampire Amish over to Methodism as soon as those Wesleyan bishops vote on the Doctrine of Transubstantiation. It's a done deal. Methodists love autoharps."

"Maybe so, but you can't be a Roman Catholic," Pedro said. "What about the crosses and the crucifixes? And the Holy Water? What about communion?"

"Not ROMAN Catholic," said Race Rankle, now as smug as a Texas school board member at a book burning. "ROMANIAN Catholic. We're going to replace those tired religious symbols with those chattering teeth you can get at

Cracker Barrel, black velvet chokers, and Halloween candy. I'll tell you this: Gluten-free wafers hold no terror for us."

"Now we shall bite thee," chanted the Vampire Amish, gnashing their gray teeth.

***

Nancy and I pulled up to Camp Daystar, née Possumtickle, and walked into the open area of the lodge that served as the community room as well as the check-in center for the Daystar Naturists of God and Love—the DaNGLs. It was cold outside, about forty degrees, and rainy, but inside the lodge it was close to seventy-five. There was no one at the desk, so Nancy pushed the buzzer. It made a loud, nasty sound and turned on a light above one of the doors. A few seconds later, a woman came in and we realized why the thermostat was set so high.

"Good morning," she chirped cheerfully, as cheerfully as any extremely plump, middle-aged, totally naked woman is wont to do under the circumstances. "Would you like to check in?"

"Alas, no," I said. "I'm Chief Konig. This is Lieutenant Parsky. We need to ask a few questions."

"How can I help?" said the woman. "My name is Gladys Hoover." Her voice said she was smiling. I smiled back, hoping that I was making eye contact.

I glanced over at Nancy. She was cool as a cucumber, her face a mask.

"I wonder if you could tell us who was in charge of the booth at the Halloween carnival last Saturday?"

"Well, I was there," said Gladys. "I worked from noon 'til about two. Then I had to come back to the camp. We were having a Bible Twister Contest. Sort of a break-the-ice mixer for new guests."

"New Christian Nudists?" asked Nancy.

"We had six new folks join us last weekend. They're all staying for the week."

"So how many people are in residence?" asked Nancy.

141

"Fourteen this week," said Gladys. "More will be coming in on Friday night."

"Hang on," I said. "Bible Twister?"

"Sure," said Gladys. "You know, Left Hand, Esther; Right Hand, Habakkuk. That sort of thing."

"Ah," I said, trying to purge the image of Gladys with one hand on Habakkuk, one hand on Esther and her feet firmly planted in First and Second Thessalonians. "So who would have been working at the booth when it closed up?"

"Well," said Gladys, thinking hard and scratching a place that I was fairly sure that most naked people wouldn't scratch in front of strangers. Perhaps the DaNGLs, I thought to myself, and perhaps all naturists, had a different code of what might constitute acceptable etiquette when in their natural habitat.

"Well..." she repeated, "I think it was Gina and Grover. You can go and ask them if you want. They're probably over at the dining hall having breakfast."

"Where exactly is the dining hall?" Nancy asked.

"Here," said Gladys, "let me draw you a map." She pulled a pencil from somewhere—a place I immediately decided wasn't made to keep pencils. She flipped over a "Welcome to Camp Daystar" flyer and quickly outlined some buildings connected by single line scrawls.

"You're here. Here's the dining hall. Here's one of the dorms. Here's the director's cabin." She pointed them out and labeled them quickly.

"You come on back if y'all decide you'd like to stay for a few days," she said. "God wants to see you as you are, and so do we!"

"Thanks," I said. "Catchy motto."

"I'm having my breakfast now, too, so if you'll excuse me." She smiled, then turned from the desk and walked back out the door from which she'd entered. I watched her go. Nancy watched me watch her go.

"You were staring at her," Nancy said accusingly when we'd left the lodge. "She wasn't even pretty."

"That's not my fault," I said. "Pretty's got nothing to do with it. Let's say you go to a zoo and a water buffalo wearing water wings comes right up to the fence. I mean, that's not a sight you see every day, is it? You're not going to *not* look, are you?"

"Totally different," said Nancy. "Although the water buffalo metaphor is apt. Here's a question for you, Mr. Detective."

"Shoot."

"What color was her hair?"

I thought for a moment, then shook my head and said, "I have no idea."

***

We walked into the dining hall and blundered into a breakfast theological discussion in full swing. At a round table in the middle of the room sat five people, as unfettered as God made them, with coffee cups in their hands, and concentration evident on their faces. Scattered around the tabletop were empty plates, some stacked on top of each other, saucers with empty butter and jam wrappers, and a couple of plastic bread baskets containing a few uneaten biscuits. From the look of things, breakfast was wrapping up.

"You see," said one of the naked men, "by comparing the basic perspectives of Arminianism and classic Calvinism, of course one has to conclude that most modern-day churches that cling to Calvinism in doctrine are more like Arminian-Wesleyan in practice."

"Absolutely," said an attractive older woman, sitting in her altogethers with her two elbows and ample bosom resting on the table, dangerously close, it seemed to me, to a steaming coffee pot. "As long as we agree to understand the need for balance between the extremes of either position."

"Ah, it's Chief Konig," said a third man, recognizing me as we walked up. "Remember me, Chief? Jason Bell." He started to stand, his hand extended in greeting.

"Please," I said, with all the sincerity I could muster, "don't get up." I shook his hand, then remembered Gladys' scratching and vowed to use Nancy's sanitizing lotion at the first opportunity. "It's good to umm... see you again, Rev. Bell."

Jason was a retired Methodist minister. He'd been living in St. Germaine for about a year, but I had no idea he was a nudist. I'd only met him once and might have recognized him under other, less-naked circumstances, but today I was glad he gave me his name.

"Do join us, won't you?" he said. "We'd enjoy the perspective of an Anglican. This is Marsha Dumpling." He pointed to the older woman, who smiled broadly. "She's a Lutheran pastor. The blowhard here is a professor of religion at Mercer. He's taking a sabbatical and working on his new book."

"Michael Graves at your service," said the professor, reaching to shake my hand. "Please excuse my topic of discussion, but I have to finish the outline and get it to the publisher by Christmas."

"These other two are Gina Terwilliger and Grover Dorfman," said Jason.

"I'm not here for the theology," said Grover. "I just like to look at Pastor Marsha's hooters."

Gina slugged him in the arm, laughed, and stood up to greet us. Gina, unlike Gladys, was thirtyish, trim, and fit. Grover was older, heavyset, and looked as though he worked out. The hair that might have once covered his head had migrated down into his ears where it sprouted like radishes, then across his shoulders, back, and chest. I had no doubt it had travelled even farther south. I saw Nancy bite the inside of her lip.

"Pay him no mind," Gina said. "Grover always likes to kid the clothed visitors. I'm sure he doesn't even notice Marsha's hooters." Grover gave a sharp barking laugh, obviously pleased with himself.

"I wonder if we could ask you and Grover a couple of questions?" I asked Gina. "Maybe at that table over there?" I nodded toward the far corner of the room.

"It's about that murder, isn't it?" said Grover, getting to his feet. "Well, this is exciting!" he said. "Let's go."

Grover and Gina were both wearing shower shoes. Just shower shoes. There were a couple of terry cloth robes dropped over the backs of the chairs where they'd been sitting, but they left them where they were and led the way to the other table. We excused ourselves from the others, left them to their theological quandary, and followed Grover and Gina to the far table. I'd been right about Grover's propensity towards de-evolution and was almost sure he rustled as he walked. They both sat, then looked up at us in expectation. We sat down across from them.

"So, what's the grift?" asked Grover. "The skinny? The dope?"

"Huh?" said Nancy, still possibly in shock over having to walk behind a bare-bottomed yeti. She cast her glance toward Gina's chest and made a discreet motion as if to warn her of some serious faux pax, if such a thing existed for the DaNGLs.

"What do you want to know?" asked Gina. She looked down where Nancy was staring, then idly brushed a bit of left-over scrambled egg off her breast.

I said, "Were you two the last people working at the pumpkin booth on Saturday night? Did you guys close it up?"

"Yeah," said Grover, "that was us. Luckily we got everything packed up before those zombies came into the park."

"So what time would that have been?"

"We got finished around six o'clock. Something like that," said Grover.

"That's pretty close," said Gina. "Maybe a little before six."

"Do you remember selling a pumpkin right before you closed?" I asked. "Probably after most of the people had gone."

"You know," said Grover thoughtfully, "we sold a bunch of pumpkins right before we closed up. It was weird. There were some of those vampire girls that came by. They all looked the same. Skinny." He snapped his fingers. "Wait a second," he said. "A man came up and bought a thirty pounder just as I was going to lug it to the van. He paid with a twenty and when I didn't have change, he just took the pumpkin and walked off. Didn't even wait for Gina to go and get the change from the front seat. Weird."

"I remember him," said Gina. "Was he the murderer?"

"You recall what he looked like?" asked Nancy.

Gina shook her head. "Not really. The sun had already gone down and it was kind of dark. Plus, we were kind of in a hurry, what with the Bible Twister tournament and all."

"He was sort of average," said Grover.

"Yeah," agreed Gina. "Average."

"Which way did he go with the pumpkin?" asked Nancy.

"I didn't see," said Gina.

"Me, neither," said Grover.

***

"Light brown," I said, as we walked back to the truck.

Chapter 17

"This pope ain't going to go for it," I said, eyeing the vampire Amish while pulling up my turtleneck. "You backed the wrong werehorse this time. He isn't known as 'God's Pit-Bull' for nothing. He'll pull the plug on your Vampire Parish so fast you'll think you were in the Intensive Care Unit down at the Lottery Winners Nursing Home."

"The pope won't even know what happened," Race rankled. "You think he's got nothing better to do than worry about an ancient parish in the middle of..."

There was a poof of smoke in the center of the room, much larger than the previous leaf-blower poofs, this time like maybe a '72 VW Bug with fouled plugs and a bad ring job, and that's when His Holiness showed up.

***

Dave was at the station when we returned. He'd gotten a box of bear-claws on his way in, not the ones from the Pig with the apple-pie filling, but the real ones from Yardborough's, large semicircular pastries with cuts around the outside edges evoking the shape from whence came the name: almond flavored, stuffed with dates and pecans.

"Thanks, Dave," said Nancy, taking one of the treats. "Did you happen to go by Rob Brannon's place in Newland yesterday?"

"Yesterday *was* my day off, you know," said Dave. "But yes, I went to Newland. There was no one home. I talked to a neighbor and he said that Brannon hadn't been there for about a week."

"Dave," I said, "get a recent picture of Rob Brannon and make some copies. They would have taken one when he was released. We need to show it around town. We don't even know what he looks like now."

"Got it," said Dave.

"And how was Wilkesboro?" Nancy asked, dragging out the name of Collette's new home town just ever-so-sweetly. "Did you enjoy yourself?"

Dave, unable to help himself, smiled like the cat that ate the vampire bat. "I guess," he said.

"Save it for later," I said. "Anything happen we should know about?"

"Bud called. He says he's fine and he's going back to school. He just had some things to sort out."

"Good deal," I said. "What else?"

"Elaine Hixon called. She said she had something important to show you. Her number is..." Dave stopped and looked out the front window. "Never mind," he continued. "Here she is."

Elaine opened the door and took the five steps to the counter. She had a brown package in her hand. "Ooo," she said, spotting the bear-claws. "Are these for anybody?"

"Help yourself," said Dave.

"In a sec." Elaine's face transformed in a moment from her usual animated visage to something much more serious. "Look here," she said. "I was in the choir dressing room in the sacristy. There were some surplices tossed in the corner and I was hanging them up. I don't know who tossed them there. These were extras, I think, because all the robes were hanging up and had their surplices with them."

"Point of clarification," said Dave, through half a mouthful of pastry. "For us Baptists. Surplice?"

"You know," said Elaine, trying to come up with a definition. "The white tunic thingy that we wear over the choir robes. It has sleeves... It's sort of flowy..."

"Oh, yeah," said Dave, with a nod of recognition. "Surplice. Got it."

"Anyway, I was picking up the surplices in the corner. There was some trash and this."

She put her brown package on the counter. It wasn't really a package. It was a brown leatherette fanny-pack.

"I opened it up to see whose it was," said Elaine. "I hope I didn't do anything wrong, but I really didn't even think about it. I read the driver's license and called Dave right away. I've been waiting at the church for you to come in and when I saw your truck pull up, I rushed right over."

We didn't need to see the driver's license. We all knew who it belonged to.

Flori Cabbage.

***

I dumped the fanny-pack onto the desk, picked up the cell phone and handed it to Nancy. She flipped it open and punched a couple of buttons.

"It's dead," she said.

"Well, charge it up," I said.

"Not that easy," said Nancy. "Cell phone manufacturers all use different chargers. This is an LG. I don't even know anyone that has an LG. We might have to order one."

"Or," I said, speaking very slowly, "Dave could go over to her apartment and... get... hers."

"Oh, yeah," said Nancy. "I guess that'd be easier."

"On my way," said Dave, picking up a second bear-claw before hitting the door.

There was nothing else of interest in the pack. A granola bar, her set of keys, her driver's license in a black slipcase, a package of tissues, a comb, some Burt's Bees lip balm, a small embroidered coin purse with some bills stuck in it. Elaine helped herself to a bear-claw. I thanked her and she left the station, looked both ways, then crossed the street and headed across the park toward St. Barnabas.

"So where's Rob Brannon?" said Nancy.

"I don't know, but I don't like this. Not one little bit. Why would he have killed Flori Cabbage? So what if she knew him from Charlotte?"

"Maybe she had something on him," Nancy said. "He's only been in prison for four years. There are a lot of crimes he'd still be liable for. In fact, most all of them. The statute of limitations is seven years."

"If she did, I think she'd have given him up long ago. No reason to wait."

"Let's say that he had some stolen money in a bank account—a lot of money. Money that Flori Cabbage knew about. If they had been involved, she might have thought that they'd get back together when he got out of prison and split the take. Then she saw Rob Brannon in Boone, realized he'd gotten out and hadn't called her, and told Ian about it."

"That's a plausible scenario," I said.

"When Brannon got out, he decided that he didn't want to split that money with Flori Cabbage, but he also knew that if he didn't share the loot, she'd turn him in. He killed her and put the pumpkin on her head in case she was discovered prematurely, thus giving him time to ransack her apartment and steal the laptop, figuring that any info that Flori had concerning him would be on it."

"Brilliant," I said. "One thing. What was Flori's fanny-pack doing in the choir dressing room at St. Barnabas?"

"Umm..." said Nancy, thinking. "I've no idea."

"And where are Bud and Elphina?"

"Huh," said Nancy.

"And why was Dr. Ian Burch, PhD, really wearing garlic?"

Nancy looked at me, confusion clouding her face.

"I was just kidding about that last one," I said. "The phone?"

Nancy nodded. "The phone."

***

Dave came back into the police station about an hour later. "Sorry," he said. "It took me this long to find the stupid thing. Her place was upside down. Know where I finally found it?"

"I couldn't care less, Dave," said Nancy, taking it from his hand. She plugged it into an outlet and stuck the round nib into the bottom of the phone. It beeped, the screen turned a bright fluorescent blue and a message came up. "Please enter your password."

"Dammit!" said Nancy. "Hang on. I can do a carrier search and find out what company she uses. What's her phone number?"

"I have no idea," I said. "Look on Ian's phone. It's on my desk."

Nancy got the phone, returned to her computer and banged on the keyboard for a minute, then gave us the info.

"U.S. Cellular," she said. "We'll need a warrant to get her password, though."

"I'll call Judge Adams," I said.

***

That afternoon, we had a warrant in hand and a promise from U.S. Cellular to get back to us as soon as possible, or if this is an emergency, please hold for the next available operator.

Chapter 18

Marilyn had finished the bulletin and I'd gone to the church to look it over before it was printed. Friday mornings were usually slow for the police force. Oh, who was I kidding? Every morning was sort of slow: that is, unless we had a murder, and we seemed to have plenty. Anyway, Friday mornings were my mornings to practice. I never did get in as much organ practice as I'd like, or maybe that was just the standard line for a part-time organist happy to play most of the notes.

I walked from Marilyn's office into the church by way of the sacristy and saw Carol Sterling at the sink, busily preparing communion for Sunday. She looked up from her work and waved. Beside her, on the floor, were two large cardboard boxes of books. I bent over, picked one up, and blew some dust off the cover. Book of Common Prayer, 1928.

"We're using these Sunday?" I asked.

"Yep. Clarence is supposed to put them into the pews."

Carol had the flatbread wafers out on the counter in a giant ziplock bag. The wafers were made by a group of women in the church that saw it as their ministry. No Styrofoam communion wafers for us. Carol had also brought in two bottles of the wine we used for communion from the storage closet in the kitchen. In the old church, the closet had a lock that could be picked by any competent first grader. We'd had that problem fixed when the church was rebuilt.

Carol took the wine opener, one of those fancy new ones, inserted the needle straight through the cork, pressed once on the top of the low pressure propellant cartridge and, pop, the cork eased out of the bottle like a Baptist out the side door of a Bingo parlor.

"Neat, eh? The only downside is that you have to rinse it off every time before you use it."

"I definitely am going to get one of those," I said.

"I'm going to need another bottle of wine. Will you get me one?" She dug in the pocket of her apron and came up with a key on a pink ribbon. "Here you go. Bring me back the key."

"Sure. No problem."

***

Mattie Lou Entriken, Wynette Winslow and Wendy Bolling were cleaning out the refrigerator, one of two industrial giants that seemed to hold as much food as a refrigerated truck. Elaine Hixon was standing warily behind them.

"Here," said Mattie Lou, pulling her head out of the fridge. "You two do something with these, will you?" She greeted me with a plate of something that might once have been tuna salad. She handed the other one to Elaine.

"Eew," said Elaine, holding her plate at arm's length. "Is that hair? Is this tuna salad growing hair? This is like an advertisement for 'The Hair Club for Men!'"

"Well," said Wynette, "it *has* been in there for a few months. It was in the back, behind that Fourth of July sheet cake."

"I'll just set mine here in the sink," I said. "Before it develops sentient thought. The garbage disposal should take care of this nicely."

"Take mine, too," said Elaine walking her plate over to me. "Anyone who doesn't believe in evolution never saw this."

"Here," said Mattie Lou, handing me two plastic covered bowls filled with macaroni and cheese. "Put these in the freezer, will you? Behind those boxes of coffee."

I went over to the freezer, opened it up, and put them behind the two big boxes labeled 'Kopi Luwak Coffee.' There was a hand-lettered sign taped to one of the boxes: *All Saints' Day. Given in memory of our beloved Junior Jameson. Keep frozen until ready to use.*

"Hey," I said, closing the door of the freezer behind me as I came out. "Coffee from Kimmy Jo Jameson. That's a nice gesture."

153

Junior Jameson was a race car driver who had ties to St. Barnabas. We'd blessed his race car right up into the NASCAR "Top Ten" before a tragic accident on the track cut his life short. His wife, Kimmy Jo, although now remarried, always made the pilgrimage to St. Barnabas at least once a year.

"Yes, sir," said Mattie Lou. "Kimmy Jo's a sweetheart. The boxes were on the counter last week when we came in. We put them right into the freezer."

"Hey, you know who helped us with it?" said Wynette. "It was that girl who got herself killed. Cabbage something. She'd come by looking for the fellow with the ears and the nose. You know, Ol' Snorty."

I laughed. "Dr. Ian Burch, PhD."

"If you say so," said Wynette. "Anyway, those boxes weren't light and you know with my back..."

"*Your* back?" said Mattie Lou. "What about *my* back?"

"I need to get a bottle of communion wine," I said.

"Help yourself," said Elaine. "You have the key?"

"Yep." I twirled the key on my finger. "Carol gave it to me."

"No more chit-chat," said Wendy, sticking her head back into the refrigerator. "We gotta get busy. Wynette, hand me that paint scraper."

***

I went up to the choir loft and played through Bach's D major fugue, my postlude for Sunday, and one of the staples of my now-dwindling repertoire. I'd learned the piece in college and it had been 'under my fingers,' as they say, for thirty years. I played through the subject, first in D, then in the relative minor, then the mediant minor. Playing a Bach fugue was like walking through a house admiring the architecture. You'd go into one room, stay for a moment or two, then wander into another room. By the time you were finished, you'd experienced the whole structure. Even if you didn't know exactly what was going on, the beauty was still there and you could appreciate it for what it was. Knowing how it was built made it that much more fun. Playing Bach also helped me think. I finished the piece, pulled out my cell phone and dialed Kent Murphee's office.

"Morgue," said Kent when he answered. "You stab 'em, we slab 'em."

"Hey, how about some professionalism? You should say 'Watauga County Coroner.'"

"What do you want?" said Kent. "I'm extremely busy."

"More dead bodies?"

"This is Boone, not St. Germaine. If you must know, I've got a poker game going in the autopsy room and I'm looking at aces over tens."

"You wish. Anyway, I know how Flori Cabbage was killed. Can I come down?"

"I was just about to call you," said Kent. "Well, right after I've skinned these EMTs and sent them home without their alligator wallets."

"Yeah? Why?"

"I finally got the tox screen back from the lab. She had traces of tetrodotoxin in her blood. It didn't kill her, but there certainly is something funny going on."

"How about this afternoon?" I said.

"See you then."

Chapter 19

I walked into the coroner's office, brown bag in hand, just as Kent Murphee was bidding his poker buddies farewell. I knew two of them. EMTs. Their expressions told it all. Mike's face was long enough to wrap twice around his neck and Joe gave "hangdog expression" a whole new meaning. I had no idea who the fourth guy was, but he seemed to have fared no better.

Kent had his pipe clenched between his teeth and was smiling broadly. "C'mon in," he chirped. "These boys were just leaving."

They grumbled past me on the way to the front door and once outside, with the door shut firmly behind them, huddled together and started gesturing at each other in an accusatory fashion. I turned and followed Kent into his office carrying my package with me.

"Just look at this," I said, starting to open the bag.

"Hang on," said Kent. "Business before pleasure. Or is it the other way around? No matter... it's four o'clock and I'm up seven hundred dollars. Cocktail time."

"I think we're going to have an intervention for you, Kent," I said. "All your friends."

"Friends? I have no friends."

I laughed. "Nothing for me, thanks, but don't let my temperance stop you."

"I can assure you that it won't," said Kent, pulling open his bottom desk drawer and coming up with a bottle of bourbon. He spit in a tumbler sitting on his desk, mopped it out with his handkerchief, and poured himself two fingers of Maker's Mark.

"I thought you were onto port," I said.

"That's my breakfast drink," said Kent. "Have you no couth?" He nodded toward my package. "Now, let me see what you have there."

I opened the bag and pulled out the gas-powered wine opener that I'd picked up in the sacristy of St. Barnabas.

"Ah, I've seen those," said Kent. "I almost bought one. You think someone plunged that needle into the victim's neck, eh?"

"I do," I said. "Then gave her a double shot of carbon dioxide. One in each of the holes."

"You pull any prints?"

I shook my head. "Nope. The church ladies wash it every time before they use it. Standard procedure."

"Well, that'd kill her, sure enough," said Kent, leaning back in his leather office chair and dropping both his feet onto the desk. He took a long puff and the scent of apple and tobacco filled the office. A good smell. It made me think that I might switch from cigars to pipes. "Say, if that is the murder weapon, may I keep it? I mean, you won't want to be using it back at the church..."

"Fine with me," I said. "Providing we don't need it as evidence."

"Well, if you're right, I'd never find any trace of the gas embolism it probably produced. It might have travelled to her heart and caused the infarction, or it might have travelled to her brain before causing the infarction. Either way, the CO2 would have dissipated long before I got around to discovering the cause." He took a sip of his drink. "Very clever," he conceded. "So you want to check and see if the needle holes fit the murder weapon."

"Yep," I said. "What do you think?"

He lifted his feet off the desk, put his lit pipe in his pocket and picked up his drink. "C'mon."

I followed him into his morgue and waited for him to open the vault containing Flori Cabbage's body. He tugged the tray out of the vault with some effort, since he was performing the task one-handed, then slid the sheet down to her breastbone. "Here," he said, passing me his drink and taking the wine opener from my hand. "Switch."

He walked across the room, retrieved a large illuminated magnifying glass on a wheeled stand, and rolled it over to the body. Then he switched on the light and held the needle close to the holes in Flori Cabbage's neck, comparing the diameter.

"We'll never be able to say for sure," he finally said, "because there are no trace substances around the wounds, and, of course, now her skin has shrunk a good bit and she's lost a fair amount of fluid. If you'll look closely, you can see that these holes in her neck are noticeably smaller than they were when she came in. Trying to match the holes with the needles just isn't going to work. How'd you come up with this theory, anyway?"

"We found Flori's fanny-pack in the choir dressing room in the sacristy. This was sitting just outside on the counter."

"If it's any consolation," said Kent, "I don't doubt you have the murder weapon here. I just don't think you can prove it."

"Yeah," I said dejectedly. "Thought I had something."

"But here's some other news," said Kent brightly. "I have the tox screen report. Back to the office, Sherlock." He set the wine opener on the counter. "And gimme my drink back."

***

"See, here," he said, pushing the report across the desk to me. "Like I told you on the phone. Flori Cabbage's blood had traces of tetrodotoxin, also known as tetrodox, also known as 'zombie powder.' It's a potent neurotoxin with no known antidote."

"Zombie powder? You're kidding me?"

"Nope. The poison is found in many widely differing animal species, including pufferfish, newts, toads, the blue-ringed octopus, trigger-fish... well, you get the idea." Kent pulled his pipe out and puffed it back to life.

"Yeah, I do. Fugu. Deadly pufferfish sushi. But we don't have a sushi place in St. Germaine."

"There was no sushi in her stomach," said Kent. "It wasn't pufferfish."

"Did she have enough in her body to kill her?"

"I don't think so, but we'll never know for sure. She would have been pretty sick at the very least, and probably paralyzed from the toxin, but sometimes people don't succumb. They have sort of a natural immunity. She wasn't alive long enough to find out."

"Huh?"

"She'd been dosed with the poison, but that wasn't what killed her. She'd probably been only recently exposed. Sometimes this

158

stuff can take up to four hours, but most people feel the effects within thirty minutes. It may be that she hadn't even felt any effects from it before she died. She died of a heat attack."

"Would this zombie powder cause her to be immobile? You know... paralytic?"

"It most certainly could have."

"So, if she was immobile, someone could have easily stuck the corkscrew in her neck and finished her off."

"Yep, but it's a stretch if you're thinking about premeditation. No one would be able to calculate when that drug might take effect, or how efficacious the dosage was." Kent looked up at the ceiling and studied the pattern his pipe smoke was making. "Well," he said, "maybe a Voodoo priest in a zombie movie could have figured it out, but it would have been much easier just to give her ten cc's of the stuff and kill her quickly."

"Hmm. Yeah, you're right. How do you think she got dosed?"

"I have no idea," said Kent. "Maybe ingestion, maybe injection. You can smoke it. You can even get it from skin contact, although it's not as potent. It's a nasty compound, a hundred times more powerful than potassium cyanide. I looked it up and the stuff is quite interesting from a medical perspective. For example, did you know that the poison isn't produced by the animals themselves, but by certain symbiotic bacteria that live inside them? Here's another thing. When it's not refrigerated, the poison loses its potency within a few hours. TTX has proven useful in the treatment of pain and was originally used in Japan in the 1930s for such diverse problems as terminal cancer, migraines, and heroin withdrawal."

"Great," I said. "Now gimme something that'll help."

"That stuff about zombie powder putting you in a deathlike trance where you're still alive but can't move," said Kent. "It ain't a myth."

Chapter 20

I cracked my knuckles, put a new piece of paper in the typewriter, and stuck my new pipe between my teeth. Raymond Chandler smoked a pipe and Raymond Chandler was the man who said, "She had a face like a collapsed lung." Meg hadn't put the kibosh on pipe smoking in the house, but only because I hadn't tried it. I wasn't ready for that kind of hairsplitting yet, so my pipe was unlit although packed with a wonderful smelling tobacco that Kent had given me called Black Cordial. Meg had spent the night at her mother's house and I'd made plans to meet her in town later for lunch, but for now, I had a free morning, a cup of coffee on the desk, and an ardent and demanding muse. I was even thinking seriously about putting on pants.

The pope floated in the air like a five-foot-tall glowing weather balloon filled with bad weather, his arms outstretched, and lightning bolts rocketing out of his fingertips. His white pointy hat shot sparks into the air like old Aunt Millie's toaster, which had also been white due to it being a 1948 model with a white enamel finish which was all the rage that year until the sparks started several house fires including the one that sent Aunt Millie to heaven, which brought us back to the pope, who also sent people to heaven, but not vampires.

"Vos bardus lamia!" he screeched in ecclesiastical fury. "Vamoosia!"

"Oooch! Oooch!" hooted the Vampire Amish in their funny Pennsylvania-Dutch dialect as they burst into flames.

Race Rankle ran for the stairs, but couldn't go fast enough, even at vampire speed, which according to many teen vampire novels is much faster than regular speed, to escape the pope's fiery finger of fate.

"Hasta la vista, Baby," the pope snarled, exhibiting both his linguistic proficiency and cinematic recall while at the same time showing off his pope superpowers by shooting Race with one of his lightning finger-bolts. "See you in purgatory."

Race went up like a Roman candle, which was sort of ironic seeing that we were, in fact, surrounded by real Roman candles, not the kind that Race Rankle went up like, which was the exploding Chinese kind, but rather the religious non-exploding kind.

"That's some real good writing," I thought to myself. I took a swallow of coffee, bit down on the pipe stem, and followed the dream.

Tessie cowered in the corner like Lindsay Lohan at a drug testing facility. "Please! Not me," she exclaimed. "I have so much to live for. I'm the one o'clock weather girl on Channel Two..."

The pope clapped his hands together with a thunderclap and the last of the vampires (which, in case you weren't paying attention, was Tessie) disappeared in a brilliant flash of light in the exact way the "Left Behind" books worked except oppositely since Tessie obviously wasn't bound for heaven, and, just like "Left Behind," she apparently had to go naked since all her clothes were piled in a smoking heap, her drawers on top, her thong now unthung.

"Naked, eh?" said Pedro. "Peeled and punished. That's gonna sting when she sits down on that brimstone."

"I did not send her to hell," said the pope, now twirling slowly like a phosphorescent piñata and fading from sight. "I sent her to Des Moines."

"Even worse," muttered Pedro.

***

While getting dressed, I decided that Baxter might like a drive into town. It was easy to take him with me as he liked nothing more than to guard the police station while I completed my chores, cheerfully slobbering on whoever might blunder into his compass. When I asked him if he wanted to go, he was out the back door and had both paws on the tailgate of the truck before I'd even cleared the kitchen. I left a baby squirrel on the window sill for Archimedes, let Baxter into the back of the pickup, and set off toward St. Germaine. It was overcast and cold, but the rain had let up for the present, so Baxter was perfectly happy hanging his face out the side of the pickup and enjoying the blast of icy wind in his teeth.

I'd told Nancy about my meeting with Kent Murphee yesterday afternoon, but she'd had no more insight than I, and I drove into town trying to put the pieces of the puzzle together. Why would Rob Brannon have killed Flori Cabbage? There had to be a reason, but I didn't know what it might be. He had to be involved somehow. The coincidences were too many. What about Ian? He had no apparent motive. Collette? I didn't think so.

Nancy was in the office when we arrived and Baxter bounded up to her, tail wagging, all kisses and snuggles. She returned his affection.

"U.S. Cellular finally called back," she said, scratching Baxter behind his ears. He closed his eyes and rumbled his appreciation. "I talked to legal and faxed the warrant. They're emailing Flori Cabbage's password in a few minutes."

"Great."

"Also, Dave left these pictures for us. Rob Brannon. They were taken last month at the prison when he was released."

Nancy pushed one of the photos across the counter toward me. It was the picture of a hard man, balding with a full beard and mustache. Rob Brannon had lost a significant amount of weight in prison and looked as though, judging by the muscles in his neck, he'd been working out. I don't think I would have recognized him had I not known who it was.

"He doesn't even look like himself, does he?" said Nancy.

"Nope. Show this around, will you? Someone might have seen him. Maybe that Grover guy who sold the pumpkin, or one of the other DaNGLs, might recognize him."

"Will do, boss."

162

"Okay," I said, scratching Baxter under his chin. "I'm taking the big guy over to the church and running through my prelude for tomorrow. I didn't get to it yesterday morning."

"Bring him back when you're finished," said Nancy. "I'll take him for a walk during lunch."

***

Nancy was waiting at the station when I finished. I could see her through the plate glass window as Baxter and I came across Sterling Park. The leaf-followers had disappeared. The rush was over and not many tourists were interested in seeing drab, soggy foliage drop from the trees in sodden clumps. I opened the door and Baxter greeted Nancy as though he hadn't seen her in three months, even though we'd left the office about a half-hour before. Nancy, of course, reciprocated.

"Just look at this," Nancy said. Baxter laid down at her feet as she held up Flori Cabbage's phone. It was open and charged and the screen was dialed up to show her texts.

"These only go back a couple weeks," said Nancy. "She must have deleted the earlier ones."

"Can we get them if we need them?"

"Phone company says no. They're gone."

"What about that thing you told Ian? You know... how we all left an electronic trail."

"Bunk," said Nancy. "Unless you've saved it, it's in the wind."

"Why doesn't this happen to the 'CSI' guys?" I asked. "They *always* have the texts."

Nancy laughed. "Yeah. They have 3-D air touch-screens, too. And they can do a DNA test in two minutes. Why do you even watch those shows?"

"To keep up," I said.

"Anyway," Nancy said, scrolling through the phone, "Wednesday, October 25th, 9:13 AM. Text from Bud: Great to meet you. Can we get 2gether this WK?"

"Text back to Bud from Flori Cabbage: BB 1?"

163

"Text back to Flori from Bud: OK."

"So they met at the Bear and Brew at one o'clock," I said. "The Wednesday before she was killed."

"Yep. Then there's a bunch of texts to various people. Nothing interesting except the ones we've already seen back and forth from her to Ian Burch."

"Skip those," I said.

"Right. Here's one to Collette on Thursday, October 26th: C U soon. Can't wait."

"Probably talking about the book signing at Eden Books."

"That's my thought," said Nancy. "Then two more from Ian and a picture of Flori Cabbage that she sent back to him that I'm gonna sell to Dave for about a million bucks. Here's one from Bud. Still Thursday, 4:10 PM: Can we meet? She answers: Sure. BB 6? Bud replies: OK."

"Be good to know what they were meeting about."

"There's more," said Nancy. "Friday, October 27, 2:32 PM from Bud: Need 2 see you B4 I go back. Flori texts back: Off at 3. Come to the house. 187 Pecan over the garage."

"Oh, man," I said. "What did Bud get into?"

"One more from Flori Cabbage to Collette on Friday at 7:12: Best day ever. Fill you in tomorrow."

"After she hooked up with Bud."

"Oh, yeah," said Nancy. "Then on Saturday, those texts and pictures between her and Ian Burch including the one at 5:32: At EB in line. Meet me later. Still freaked." Nancy looked up at me. "Then... the kicker."

I waited for it.

"On Saturday at 5:47, fifteen minutes later, she sent Bud a text: Meet me in the sacristy. Something to show U."

"During the movie," I said.

"During the movie."

"Let's find Bud after lunch," I said. "I kinda doubt he went back to school."

***

I met Meg for lunch at the Ginger Cat. Annie Cooke greeted us, led us to a table, and put two menus down in front of us.

"Not much business today," she said sadly. "I might as well close up for a month."

I offered her my best sympathetic smile. "What are the specials?" I asked.

"I can't remember," she said. "Anyway, I'm not the waitress. In fact, your waitress isn't even a waitress." She laughed at her own joke.

"Huh?" I said.

She was right. Up flounced Christopher Lloyd—"Mr. Christopher" as he was known to his customers and devotees.

"Mr. Christopher!" Meg said. "I didn't know you were working here. How lovely!"

"It's just for a few months," said Mr. Christopher, placing glasses of water in front of each of us. "As you know, there were some problems with my TV show. The cable network just couldn't accept my lifestyle."

"Ah, I see," said Meg sympathetically. "You would have thought that a design show might have taken your lifestyle into account."

"You'd have thought," sniffed Mr. Christopher. "Anyway, I'd already sold my interior design business in Boone, so I guess I'm starting from scratch. No matter." He struck a pose: elbows in, wrists out, feet in third position. "Here I am," he tweedled. "How may I serve you?"

Contrary to his public stance on the reason for his dismissal, everyone in Watauga County knew that Mr. Christopher had been doing very well with his show, *The 14 Layers of Style,* until he had been captured on video *in flagrante delicto* with a rather robust cameraman and the cameraman had decided that he would "come out" by posting it on the internet. Even HGTV couldn't keep Mr. C on the air after that.

"What is the special, Mr. Christopher?" asked Meg, perusing the menu, but not really looking. The menu was superfluous. I knew she'd order the special.

"Today we're featuring sesame-crusted, pan-seared tuna, potatoes, *haricots verts*, heirloom tomatoes, black olives, and capers in a mustard vinaigrette."

"What the heck is a *haricots verts*?" I said.

"Shh," said Meg, hushing me. "They're French green beans. *Please!*"

Mr. Christopher rolled his eyes. Meg joined him. They rolled their eyes at me for a while, then Meg said, "That sounds wonderful," and closed her menu.

Mr. Christopher changed his ballet stance from third position to fifth and swiveled in my direction. "And for you, Chief? Might I interest you in the Boeuf à la Stroganoff: red wine braised beef short ribs with house-made buckwheat noodles, wild mushrooms, and porcini cream?" He pointed to my menu. "It's right there on the second page."

"Nah," I said. "I think I'll have a fried egg sandwich."

Meg, who was taking a sip of water at the time, sprayed half a mouthful across the table before her napkin made it to her lips.

By the time our meals had arrived (I couldn't help but notice that Mr. Christopher had managed to dress my egg sandwich up with some of those capers—either that, or there was a rabbit loose in the kitchen), Cynthia Johnsson, our erstwhile mayor and Pete's significant other, had come in with her two nieces, one of them being Addie Buss and the other, Addie's younger cousin, Penny Trice. Penny was seven.

"Good afternoon, ladies," I said.

"Hi, you guys," added Meg.

"We've just been petting Baxter," said Penny. "He was outside with... umm..."

"Lieutenant Parsky," said Cynthia.

"Yes, ma'am," said Penny. "Lieutenant Parsky. He's quite a good dog."

166

"Thank you, Penny," said Meg. "He *is* a good dog. Maybe you'd like to come up to our house and play with him sometime."

"Oh, yes," said Penny. "Yes, I would like that very much."

"Can I come, too?" said Addie.

"*May* I come, too?" corrected Cynthia.

"*May* I come, too?" repeated Addie.

"Absolutely!" said Meg with a big smile.

"What are you having for lunch?" asked Cynthia. "It looks delicious."

"Fried egg sandwich," I said, with my mouth half-full.

"Not you," said Cynthia, half-disgusted. "I was asking Meg." Then she and Meg engaged in a pother of eye-rolling. Then Mr. Christopher walked by and rolled *his* eyes. Then the two girls rolled *their* eyes. I vowed to never eat at the Ginger Cat again.

***

Meg and I were walking back to the station when a text popped up on my phone. It was from Pauli Girl. It said, "Come to the house PDQ."

Chapter 21

I drove my truck up to Coondog Holler with Nancy in the front seat. Meg had packed Baxter into her Lexus and driven back to the house. We turned up the McCollough's drive and ended up right behind Bud's Nissan station wagon, blocking it in. It had been packed to the top of the windows and there was a bundle tied up with a tarp lashed to the roof. Nancy and I exited our vehicle, walked up onto the porch and knocked on the door. Pauli Girl was the one who answered. Frowning, she opened the door all the way and gestured us in. Bud was sitting at the kitchen table, his head in his hands. I walked over to the table and sat down. Nancy took a quick and unobtrusive tour of the trailer.

"Wow, Bud. You want to tell me what's going on?"

Bud looked up. There were tears on his cheeks. "I guess I'd better tell you," he said. "How'd you know I was here?"

"I'm a detective, Bud," I said, shooting Pauli Girl a look. "We found Flori Cabbage's phone. Your texts were all there."

"Oh," he said.

"No one else here," said Nancy.

"Where's Elphina?" I asked.

"She'll be back in a little while," said Bud softly, his eyes now focused on the table. Pauli Girl flicked her glance toward the back door. I gave a small nod.

"Listen, Bud, I know she's the one who killed Flori Cabbage. I just want to know why."

If Nancy was surprised, she didn't show it.

"We were going to go to Florida," Bud said. "Start a new life. Elphina said she knew some guys who had a house in Pensacola where we could stay for a while."

"Bud, it's never a good plan to run away," I said. "What about your dream? What about college? Moosey? Your mom? Your sister? There are people here that depend on you." I glanced up at Pauli Girl. She smiled a small, very sad smile.

Another tear ran down Bud's cheek. "I know. I just love her. She said we'd be together."

"Well, tell me what happened."

"How did you know?"

"We found the murder weapon," Nancy said, as if this explained it. "The wine opener."

Bud nodded and began his story.

***

"I met Flori Cabbage last week, the week I was on fall break. Well, I'd seen her around, but I never spoke to her. I went into the Appalachian Music Shoppe just to look around and she and I got to talking. Did you know she had a photographic memory?"

"Yeah," I said.

"And that she spoke like seven languages?"

"We knew."

"Well, I told her that I had taken those wine courses during the summer and she said that she'd read this treatise on wine in Paris when she'd been in France on vacation. She said one afternoon, she wandered into the Bibliothèque Nationale and somehow ended up in the manuscript room. She pulled this one folio out, just at random, sat down, and started reading it just for something to do. It was the treatise I told you about, the one by Gilbert Rabelais. It's an amazing document and will set the wine community on its ear when it's published."

"I remember your telling me about it."

"So I met her three or four times after that. Flori said she was happy to tell me what was in the book. She'd repeat whole sections of the text, like she was reading it off the page and translating the French at the same time. It was amazing. I'd record her on my cell phone, then I'd go home and transcribe it. I have it stuck in the car somewhere."

"So what happened on Saturday. A week ago."

"I was at the movie. You asked me to help with the DVD player."

"Right," I said.

"So I was watching the movie and maybe about halfway through, I get a text from Flori. It said that she had something to show me in the sacristy. I thought it was related to what we were working on. You know, the Rabelais treatise. So I snuck down the aisle and into the sacristy. It was that part in the movie where everyone is running around in the dark, so it was easy to do without anyone seeing me. At least that's what I thought."

"How did Flori know you'd be in the church?"

"I guess she knew I'd be going to see *Nosferatu*. She was sort of into the vampire thing. I invited her to come along, but she said she was going to the book signing."

"So someone saw you leaving the movie?" Nancy asked.

"Yeah," said Bud sadly. "Elphina saw me. She was really excited to meet Salena Mercer. She was in line at the bookstore, but after waiting a while, she decided to come over to the church. She got some girl to save her place."

"So she was in the church and saw you get up and go into the sacristy." I said. "Why wasn't she sitting with you?"

"She didn't know where I was. The church was packed and she came in late. She saw me when I got up."

"So she followed you?" said Nancy.

"Yeah. I walked into the sacristy and all the lights were out, but there was one on in the choir dressing room. The door was mostly closed. I thought Flori Cabbage might be there, so I pushed the door open. She was there all right and she had no clothes on at all. She was naked and she smiled and did this!" Bud crooked his finger in a "come-over-here" gesture. "It sort of freaked me out 'cause I didn't know what was going on! I mean, I had no idea. I thought we were friends and that she was just helping me out."

He stopped talking for a moment, then said, "May I have a drink of water?"

"Sure," I said. Pauli Girl went to the sink, filled a jelly jar with some water and set it on the table in front of Bud. He picked it up and took a long swallow.

"I came out of the dressing room," continued Bud, "and like I said, I was pretty freaked. I was just trying to get out of there. I went out the back door instead of the one leading back into the church. When I tried to get back in, it was locked. I had to go all the way around and come back in the front. Then I went back to my seat and sat for the rest of the movie."

"Did Elphina tell you exactly what happened when she found Flori Cabbage in the dressing room?" Nancy asked.

"Yeah," said Bud. He took a couple of deep breaths followed by another sip of water. "She told me that she saw me leave the movie and after a couple of minutes came after me. She heard a noise in the dressing room and got sort of scared, so she pulled out her stun gun. She's got one that looks like a flashlight." He shrugged. "She always carries it."

"Then she saw Flori Cabbage without her clothes and thought the worst," said Nancy.

"Well, by that time, she had some of them back on," said Bud. "Elphina knew I was meeting with her. She said that Flori was after me, but I didn't believe her! She was so mad because she loves me so much..."

"So she zapped her with the stun gun," said Nancy, "right in her neck. Then used the wine opener to finish her off and cover up the marks the stun gun made."

"Yes."

Nancy continued: "Dressed her, dragged her out the back, put her in the hay maze, and stuck a pumpkin on her head."

"She didn't tell me about the pumpkin."

"How'd she manage the rest?" asked Nancy. "She wasn't a big girl."

"She's strong," said Bud. "No kidding. I once saw her carry a full keg of beer up a flight of stairs."

"Where have you two been staying?" I asked.

"In the car. Elphina kept trying to get hold of her friends in Florida, but never did. She finally decided that we should just go." Bud put his head on the table and his shoulders shook.

I gave Bud a minute, then said, "You got a text after the movie was over. Outside on the steps. What did it say?"

Bud didn't answer, but reached into his pocket, pulled out his phone, and handed it to me. I passed it over to Nancy. It took her just a moment to pull up the text.

"You won't be seeing your slut again. We're both dead," she read.

Pauli Girl bristled. "I hate that Mary Edith Lumpkin," she said.

***

We told Bud he was not to leave the county, and that it would be a good idea for him and Pauli Girl to follow us back into town. They could come and stay with Meg and me tonight. Bud went to the bathroom to clean up. Pauli Girl walked with us to the front door.

"She left when she saw you driving up," she whispered. "Out the back, into the woods."

"Yeah," I said. "We know. Thanks for the text. I won't tell Bud."

"What's going to happen to him?"

"Nothing," I said. "He hasn't actually broken any laws. It's a good thing we got here when we did."

"What about aiding and bedding a fugitive?" Pauli Girl asked, obviously as big a fan of the crime shows as I.

Nancy hid a smile behind a fake cough. "Well, she wasn't a fugitive 'til right now," she said. "He did have knowledge of a crime already committed, but that's not a criminal offense unless we ask him about it and he lies. Then we might have reason to charge him with obstruction. Right now, though, it's all on Elphina."

"Don't worry," I said. "We'll find her."

"I ain't worried," said Pauli Girl, her eyes narrowing. "I'd just as soon stay here. She comes back and *no one* will have to worry about her anymore."

"I know. That's why I want you two to stay with us tonight. We'll take all the vehicles with us."

***

Nancy and I waited by the truck while the two kids got what they needed to spend the night.

"What a bluffer," said Nancy with a grin. "Admit it! You had no idea that Elphina was the murderer when we came up here."

"Well, that's true enough," I said. "I had the thought when I saw the packed car. Even then, I was fishing."

"You're a good angler, Chief."

"You're pretty good yourself," I said.

Chapter 22

Bud and Pauli Girl accompanied Meg and me to church on Sunday morning. Meg had fixed us all breakfast before we left, and we'd dined on homemade biscuits, bacon, apple butter, and various jams that she'd bought at the Ginger Cat before she'd left yesterday.

St. Barnabas was abustle. Moosey came running up to us when we walked into the parish hall and he threw his arms around Pauli Girl.

"Hi, Pauli Girl!" he bubbled. "Hi, Bud. Hey! Lookit what I've got!" He reached into his front pocket and started to pull something out, but Bernadette was right behind him.

"Don't show!" she yelped. "It's for later."

"Oh, yeah," said Moosey, stuffing whatever it was back into his pocket. "Hey! Mama's coming home tomorrow. I like it at the Kentons', but I'll be glad to get home. Hey! Did you feed my turtle?"

"What turtle?" said Pauli Girl. "And stop saying 'Hey!'"

"He's in the toilet in Mama's bathroom," said Moosey. "I put him there for safety."

Pauli Girl made a face.

"I've got to go up to the choir loft," I said. "I'll see everyone later."

***

"I hope we get the rest of this story soon," said Marjorie. She'd gotten to the loft early, as usual. "I'm writing a review. You know. For the church newsletter."

"Endeavor to be kind," I said.

"Oh, I'm afraid I can't do that. I have my literary standards, you know."

"Yes, I know."

"I went down to the parish hall to get some of that fancy-cat coffee, but they didn't have any," grumbled Marjorie. "They only had Community Coffee. That's okay I guess, but I was really looking forward to it."

"We're having it after the service," I said.

"Ohhh," said Marjorie.

The choir started coming in and filled the chairs one by one.

"I went to my Sunday School class," said Elaine. "Guess who was there? The Congregational Enlivener. Kimberly Walnut was taking him around and introducing him. His name is Nick Duckling."

"I can't wait to meet him," I said, being in quite a good mood after the events of the previous evening. There were still many unanswered questions, but I'd be happy to tackle those tomorrow.

"Hey," said Steve. "Here are the new prayer books. I mean, the *old* prayer books."

"About time," said Marjorie.

"Let's take out our music, please," I said. "We'll go through it, but quite frankly, we may have to be flexible this morning. Kimberly Walnut and Mr. Duckling will be interjecting some fun elements into the service and they've decided that these should be a surprise."

"And our service shall be enlivened," said Elaine.

"Indeed it shall," I said. "Now let's look at that Puccini anthem."

***

The kids, Moosey's Eleven, were sitting third-row center, their Boomwhackers, or rather, their Spirit Sticks, in hand when the service started. Other younger kids had Spirit Sticks as well. Kimberly Walnut had bought fifty of them, and since there weren't fifty kids in the parish, there were a few of the strange instruments left over. It was no surprise, then, to see that all the basses had them squirreled away under their chairs.

The choir had robed and was waiting downstairs in the narthex to process. I played the prelude, then started the hymn *For All The*

Saints. I could hear the congregation singing as I played, then the individual voices of the choir as they came into the sanctuary.

> *For all the saints, who from their labors rest,*
> *Who Thee by faith before the world confessed,*
> *Thy Name, O Jesus, be forever blessed.*
> *Alleluia, Alleluia!*

> *Thou wast their Rock, their Fortress and their Might;*
> *Thou, Lord, their Captain in the well fought fight;*
> *Thou, in the darkness drear, their one true Light.*
> *Alleluia, Alleluia!*

This hymn has eight verses, and since we only sang it once a year, we sang them all. I had a couple of alternate harmonizations I used as well as Vaughan Williams', and when the sopranos took off on a descant on the last stanza, I cranked it up.

"Mr. Scott, take us to warp-nine," I heard a little voice in my head say.

"She canna take any more of this, Captain!" answered Scotty from inside the organ console. "She's gonna blow!"

I just hoped the Congregational Enlivener was enjoying himself.

> *From earth's wide bounds, from ocean's farthest coast,*
> *Through gates of pearl streams in the countless host,*
> *And singing to Father, Son and Holy Ghost:*
> *Alleluia, Alleluia!*

Benny Dawkins was absent, having been hired for a festival service at Independent Presbyterian Church in Birmingham. He'd made his apologies and left Addie Buss in charge of the smoke slinging. She did a fine job, dropping an *Ezekiel Flying Pinwheel*, a *Jonah Sinker*, and something she called *Eutychus' Death Plunge* into the mix.

Vicar McTavish had stopped on the top step, turned to face the congregation, and waited for the hymn to finish before offering the opening collect. I played the final chords and the priest waited for the majestic sound to stop reverberating through the rafters. It was a dramatic pause and a dramatic pause was called for. The priest raised his mighty arms and took a deep breath. None of us, certainly not McTavish, expected the Congregational Enlivener to jump up from the front pew, spin around and yell, "Y'all sit down! I'm Nick Duckling and we're here to *CE-LE-BRATE!*"

Nick Duckling was dressed in an orange shirt, blue-plaid pants, and bright yellow suspenders.

The vicar lowered his arms. The congregation sat down nervously.

"So, before we go any further, *let's hear it for Jesus!*"

This was the cue for all the kids to start beating their Spirit Sticks on the back of the pew in front of them. It caused quite a racket. Most of the kids figured out very quickly that smacking the person in front of them on the head made just as much noise and was a heck of a lot more fun. The basses had discovered this as well and were taking advantage of the cranial tunefulness of the tenor section.

Gimme a "J!" yelled Nick Duckling.

Kimberly Walnut and Heather Frampton, one of the St. B ex-cheerleader soccer moms that Kimberly had inveigled, jumped to their feet and yelled "J!"

"Gimme an E!"

"E!" screamed Kimberly.

"Quit smackin' me," yelped Marjorie.

The rest of the congregation sat in stunned shock.

"I was a cheerleader once," said Elaine. "He's trying to get us to spell something. I wonder what it is?"

"Gimme an S!" Nick yelled.

"SSSSS!" yelled the women, jumping up and down and looking around to see whom they were enlivening. The Boomwhackers were still whacking away, but everyone else sat frozen, not daring to move. The vicar was motionless and seemed, if anything, to be getting larger as his anger increased.

"Gimme a U!" Nick Duckling pointed the index fingers of both hands at the congregation, thus imparting his double meaning. The "U" in Jesus, referred to "you." Or rather, "us." How could we have been so blind?

"Yoooouuu!" mooed the cheering squad.

"S!" shouted Nick. "What's that spell?"

"JESUS!" shouted the two ladies.

"What's that spell?" shouted Nick again, this time louder.

"*JESUS!*" they shouted back.

Nick Duckling did a back flip in front of the chancel steps. "Let's give him a hand!" he hollered, skipping down the aisle, clapping above his head.

Kimberly Walnut and Heather jumped up and down, applauding and cheering. The kids whacked their Spirit Sticks on whatever and whomever was close. The rest of the congregation, unsure of what to do, applauded lightly for a few seconds, then quit. Even the basses seemed somewhat embarrassed.

Nick disappeared out the back, no doubt preparing for his next explosion of enlivening. The two cheerleaders looked around and seeing no one joining them in their little hops and yips of ecstasy, sat down.

All eyes went to Fearghus McTavish. His eyes were icy blue fire and he seemed to be smoldering from within. He raised his hands again, then, his voice deep and menacing, spoke the collect: "All consuming and unpitying God, who dost enkindle thy Holy name in the hearts of the Saints; Grant to us, thy lamentable servants, the same faith and power; so, as we rejoice in their triumphs, we may profit by their examples and not wallow in the filth from which we came; through Jesus Christ our Lord. Amen."

"At least he's sticking with the '28 prayer book," I said. "Although admittedly somewhat altered."

"Hear what our Lord Jesus Christ saith," the priest growled. "Thou shalt love the Lord thy God with all thy heart, and with all thy soul, and with all thy mind. This is the first and greatest commandment. And the second is like unto it; Thou shalt love thy neighbor as thyself. On these two commandments hang all the Law and the Prophets."

The '28 prayer book called for a *Kyrie* and we obliged. We were singing the last "Lord, have mercy," when Nick Duckling bounded in from the side door beside the Mary altar.

"It's time for the Children's Moment!" he cheered. "C'mon down, kids!"

The priest began to visibly sizzle. It was like one of those cartoons where smoke starts to come out of someone's ears. Like that, but scarier.

***

The small children went into the aisle, pushed out by their mothers as usual, then began the long trek down to the steps. When they were about halfway to their destination, Nick Duckling shouted out, "Not just the little ones! *All* you kids come on down! Kids of all ages!" He looked up at me, pointed a finger and called, "Mr. Music Man! Play us a little traveling music!"

I might have played *Jesus Loves Me* or something had I gotten a little advance notice, but for some reason, the only song I could think of right then was *Seasons In The Sun*. I shrugged and played a verse.

Muffy, our aspiring Karaoke star, started singing along when I got to the chorus:

> We had joy, we had fun, we had seasons in the sun;
> But the wine and the song, like the seasons, have all gone.

Moosey's Eleven, as they'd become known in the Sunday School, having graduated from being called the *Fearsome Foursome*, the *Children of the Corn*, and the *Gang of Eight*, were ready and waiting for the invitation. They'd been good so far, their little heads bowed, but their little fingers silently working. Now they stood and entered the aisle behind the smaller kids, their heads still down, following them to the chancel steps.

"Now, children," said Nick loudly. "How much do we love God? Do we love him *this* much?" Nick had his hands a couple feet apart.

"Yes!" yelled the little kids. The older kids kept their heads down.

"Do we love him THIS much?" The space between Nick Duckling's hands widened.

"Yea!" yelled the little kids. The older kids didn't respond.

"Do we love him THIS MUCH?" Nick stretched his arms as far as he could and one of the Douglas boys reared back and slugged him in the crotch with his fist. He bent over in surprise and pain and came face to face with eleven terrifying faces. Moosey and his friends had spent the first part of the service applying Brother Hog's *Plague Faire* favors using super-glue and the compact mirrors that had been thoughtfully provided by the Girls' Sunday School class when they had their lesson on self esteem. Now they looked up at him and smiled sweetly. The sweetness of their smiles, however, was tempered by inflamed boils with flies dipping in around the edges, open sores and wounds, warts, lesions, and a few exuding maggots. Bernadette had brought her bulging rubber eyeball back out for an encore. It went fetchingly with her frilled pink dress.

Nick Duckling took one look and screamed. Then, either from fright, the Douglas boy's right cross, or maybe a combination of both, he sat down on the steps, fell over, and curled into a fetal position. The acolytes helped him to his feet and out of the church through one of the doors to the sacristy.

The kids, all of them, turned and walked back down the aisle without a word. I was ready this time, and played:

Jesus loves the little children,
All the children of the world...

Chapter 23

"Hear the Word of the Lord!" thundered Vicar Fearghus McTavish. "For a fire is kindled in mine anger, and shall burn unto the lowest hell, and shall consume the earth with her increase, and set on fire the foundations of the mountains. They shall be burnt with hunger, and devoured with burning heat, and with bitter destruction."

"I guess that Nick Duckling made him plenty mad," whispered Meg.

"I will also send the teeth of beasts upon them, with the poison of serpents of the dust," he growled. "Now this will be the plague with which the Lord will strike all the peoples who have gone to war against Jerusalem; their flesh will rot while they stand on their feet, and their eyes will rot in their sockets, and their tongues will rot in their mouth."

"Zombies!" said Marjorie happily. "This is gonna be the best All Saints' sermon ever!"

***

The choir sang their offertory anthem very well, and by the time we were going down to the altar for communion, most of the folks had calmed down and almost seemed to have forgotten about Nick Duckling, our Congregational Enlivener. I half-expected him to come popping into the service at some point, but it wasn't to be. Perhaps Kimberly Walnut was consoling him in her office.

We went downstairs for communion, partook of the bread and wine, and listened to the words of grace from Vicar McTavish:

"Take, eat, abase your carnal nature, and hang your head in mortification."

and

"The bread of solace, the cup of consolation."

and

"Do not be deceived by false gifts. Their drink is the poison of dragons, and the cruel venom of asps."

"We rarely get communion sentences from the Book of Deuteronomy," I whispered, as Meg and I walked down the side aisle toward the stairway leading back to the choir loft.

"Come to the table as a wretched worm and contemplate God's grace."

Elaine and Bev had repaired to the parish hall as soon as the offertory was finished to help set up for coffee hour, so I was short two sopranos for the communion anthem. I was contemplating my options, Muffy and Meg being the only two left in the section, when I saw Nancy waiting for me in the narthex at the foot of the stairs. She was in her uniform, of course, and had a steely look on her face. She motioned me out the front doors and onto the steps.

"I saw Rob Brannon in town this morning," she said. "At least I think it was him. He was driving a white Ford Escort on Poplar Drive right in front of the bank. He probably saw me, too, because by the time I'd turned around, he'd taken a side street and was gone."

"Rob Brannon?" said Meg, who'd followed us out. "What's he doing in town?"

"No idea," said Nancy.

"Something's up," I said. "Is Dave working?"

Nancy shook her head. "I think that he's in Wilkesboro again."

"Well, drive around and see if you can spot Brannon again. Let's make sure it's him. Pull him over for speeding or something."

"Or something."

Meg and I went back inside and started climbing the stairs to the loft when Bev came back in the front door.

"I just saw Nancy leaving. What's going on?"

"Police stuff," I said. "What's happening in the kitchen? You're back early, not that I'm complaining. Now we can sing that Mozart motet."

"What a disaster!" said Bev, exasperation spilling from her voice. "First, the bakery doesn't have enough cinnamon coffee cakes, so they substituted chocolate walnut. Nick Duckling came into the kitchen, grabbed a plate of cannolis and cinnamon buns and took off with Kimberly Walnut. I guess they're in her office

182

licking their wounds. Then Kylie Moffit came over from Holy Grounds to help make the coffee. She's the one that ordered it for the celebration. So she comes in and found that *not only* had someone stuck the whole shipment in the freezer, but that they had stolen about two pounds of the stuff. At $350 a pound, that's seven hundred bucks!"

"Freezer? I saw the sign on the box. It said to keep it frozen."

"Apparently you don't freeze coffee beans. It messes with the flavor," said Bev with all the sarcasm of one who frequently freezes coffee beans.

"The beans were in bags?" I asked.

"One big jute bag per box filled with beans and tied with a heavy string. Seven pounds per bag. One of them was about two pounds light. Now Wynette is on a tear about putting locks on all the refrigerators and the walk-in. I *swear...*"

I remembered the words of comfort from Vicar McTavish.

"Do not be deceived by false gifts. Their drink is the poison of dragons, and the cruel venom of asps."

"Oh, jeez," I said. "Meg, go up and tell Marjorie she has to play the last hymn."

Meg looked horrified. "No," she said.

"Then everyone can sing it a cappella. I've gotta go."

"Marjorie only plays the piano," Meg said, panic in her voice. "And badly!"

But I was already running for the parish hall.

***

I burst into the kitchen to the amazement of the four women who were working. Wynette, Mattie Lou, and Elaine were busy putting pastries on silver serving platters before carrying them out to the hall and setting them on the beautifully laid tables. Kylie Moffit was working at the two coffee urns, busily transferring the coffee from the brewing urns to the carafes that would be used to serve the unique brew.

"Who drank the coffee?" I said, as I banged through the double doors.

I caught them all by surprise and they froze for a moment before Wynette said, "I don't think anyone has."

I looked to the other three women. They all shook their heads, indicating they hadn't had time to try it yet.

"Anyone touch any of the beans?"

Everyone's eyes went to Kylie. "Well, yes," she said. "I guess I did. I mean, I must have, although I poured them into the grinder right from the bag. Then I used this scoop here." She held up a measuring cup. "What's wrong?"

"Wash your hands," I said.

Kylie moved to the sink immediately and lathered up.

I pulled a picture from my pocket and showed it to her. "You recognize this guy?"

Kylie nodded but didn't speak.

"It's a good bet that the coffee beans are poisoned," I said. "We're not taking a chance and we don't need to panic everyone. Kylie, you pour it all down the drain, but save me about a cup in a sealed jar. Wynette, get a trash bag for the grounds. Don't touch them. Bag 'em up and put them back in the freezer. Wear those rubber gloves they use for washing dishes. Okay? Mattie Lou, make some more Community Coffee and throw in some stuff to make it taste a little different."

"Nutmeg and black pepper," said Kylie. I winked at her.

"Elaine, you get the rest of the food out. Everybody got it?"

They nodded, too stunned to say anything.

"Let's hurry," I said. "Go, go! And not a word about any of this to anyone. Ever. Got it?"

The women virtually leapt into action.

"Am I going to die?" said Kylie as she turned the urn over into the sink.

"Nope," I said, hoping I was telling the truth. "You'll be fine."

***

The after-service All Saints' Day celebration was a huge success, with the whole church in attendance. Kimmy Jo Jameson did not show up, but I didn't expect that she would. Meg came in, looking for answers, but I laid a finger aside my nose, our signal that all would be explained later.

The pastries were delicious, as we knew they would be, and the mock Kopi Luwak coffee was tasted by all, even the kids. Moosey and his gang were still decked out in their *Plague Faire* favors and hovering around the chocolate coffee cake table in an effort to scare the smaller children back over to the sugar cookies.

"This coffee is certainly worth the price," said Annette Passaglio. "It may be the best coffee I've ever had. I had no idea. I'm going to start ordering it."

"I can take it or leave it," said Marjorie. "I don't taste litter-box, but it's a little peppery for my taste."

"How did you do on the hymn?" I asked. "Sorry I had to take off. A bit of an emergency."

"She did fine," said Meg. "Although it was a slightly different accompaniment than we were expecting."

"In what way?" I asked.

"I didn't care for that hymn you picked," said Marjorie. "So I played one I liked."

"*Whispering Hope?*" I asked.

"Oh, no," said Meg. "That would have been refreshing. Do you happen to know *The Wreck of the Edmund Fitzgerald?*"

"Sure!" I said with a big smile. "Gordon Lightfoot. I didn't know it was a hymn."

"I know that one by heart," sniffed Marjorie. "I find it very spiritual."

Bev walked up and threw her hands up into the air. "Well, that's that!"

"What?" Meg asked.

"Vicar Fearghus McTavish resigned right after the service. He said he's done what he came to do or something like that. I can't find him anywhere. I'll bet that Nick Duckling was the last straw, or maybe that hymn. After that, the vicar didn't want any part of St. Barnabas."

Meg and I shot each other a look.

"That Kimberly Walnut!" Bev shook her head and took a sip of coffee. She made a face. "I don't know what all the fuss is about. I mean, this is good, but it's not worth twenty bucks a cup."

***

Meg, Nancy, and I sat down at our table at the Slab Café. Pete joined us as soon as we sat down and Cynthia came in a couple of minutes later. Noylene and Pauli Girl were working the floor but the church crowd had come and gone and we had the place mostly to ourselves.

"I'm going home," announced Pauli Girl, taking off her apron and tossing it into the dirty apron and napkin basket behind the counter. "Lunch is over and Mom's coming home. I've gotta go clean up the house."

"Thanks for coming in," said Pete. "See you Tuesday afternoon?"

"I'll be here," said Pauli Girl.

"How's Bud doing?" asked Meg.

"He'll be okay. He talked to the dean at the college and got squared away. He's going back tomorrow."

"That's great," said Meg. "You be careful driving home."

"Yes, ma'am," said Pauli Girl and walked out the door. The cowbell banged against the glass and registered her departure.

"So, spill it," said Meg. "What on earth happened?"

"Well, you know that Nancy saw Rob Brannon in town," I said.

"I *thought* I saw him," Nancy said. "Maybe I did, maybe I didn't. Whoever it was, he's gone now."

"Anyway," I continued, "when Bev said that Kylie Moffit was complaining about the coffee being in the freezer, I knew something was up. Here's the thing. Flori Cabbage got dosed with zombie powder..."

"Tetrodotoxin," said Nancy.

"Right," I said. "But that wasn't what killed her. She got a small dose. Something she probably got when she stole some of the beans out of the walk-in on the night she was killed."

"She stole some beans?" said Meg.

"Sure. She knew they were there and probably thought they wouldn't be missed. She helped Mattie Lou and Wynette put them into the freezer.

"But wouldn't she have had to drink it?" asked Pete.

"Nope, just digging in it with her hands would be enough. Kent doesn't think it was enough to kill her. It was probably enough to make her sick, but she hadn't had time to start feeling the effects before she was killed by Elphina."

"Then where's the coffee she stole?" asked Cynthia.

"It was right where she left it," I said. "I picked it up after the reception."

"Well...?" said Meg.

"In the choir robing room. Elaine found the fanny pack on the floor in the corner under some surplices. The coffee was in a brown paper bag in the same place. Elaine found the fanny pack and rushed it over. We never went back and looked through that trash for anything else."

"Okay," said Meg. "Back to the freezer."

"Right," I said. "So Kylie was complaining that someone put the coffee in the freezer. I saw the sign on the box. 'All Saints' Day. Given in memory of our beloved Junior Jameson. Keep frozen until ready to use.' What would be the reason to freeze the coffee? Because that zombie powder..."

"Tetrodotoxin," said Nancy.

"Right. That stuff loses its potency unless kept at a low temperature."

Pete got up and brought a coffee pot over to the table and refilled everyone's cups.

"So Rob Brannon tried to kill everyone at the church?" Cynthia asked.

"We'll check the coffee and the grounds, but that's my thought. Kylie recognized the picture of Rob Brannon. He was the one who came to pick up the coffee. I already called Kimmy Jo Jameson. She didn't send it. In fact, she had forgotten all about All Saints' Day."

"So why did he grab Flori Cabbage's computer?" asked Pete.

"He didn't," said Nancy. "Ian Burch did. I found it in the back of his shop. It has a password, and if we bother to get into it, I'm betting there are going to be a lot more pictures and emails. Stuff that Dr. Ian Burch, PhD, isn't especially proud of."

"Are you going to bother?" Meg asked.

"I doubt it," I said.

"Then why did Rob Brannon stick a pumpkin on Flori Cabbage's head after he found her dead in the hay maze?"

"It wasn't him," I said. "At least I don't think it was. I think it was Elphina. We'll ask her when we find her, but one thing was for sure. She was furious at Flori Cabbage."

"Is that everything?" asked Cynthia. "Is everything wrapped up nicely? May I give a full report to the city council?"

"No!" came the answer from the rest of the table.

***

Meg and I walked into the church after lunch and started down the aisle toward the steps to the choir loft where I'd left the organ on, and my jacket hanging on a hook. We'd gotten halfway when we heard a noise at the front. Turning around, we saw the vicar kneeling at the altar. If he spotted us, he didn't acknowledge our presence right away. After he'd finished praying, he stood, faced us, and waited for us to approach.

"We hear you're leaving us," said Meg.

"Aye," said the vicar, the brogue rolling over his lips and down the front of his black cassock. "I've done what I could. Congregational Enlivener..." He shook his head in dismay. "There's no hope for ye."

"Ah, there's always hope," I said. "Hope is what we have. Hope and grace and Kimberly Walnut."

Postlude

We had the coffee and the grounds tested and they contained, as we thought, enough Tetrodotoxin to do us all substantial harm. Kylie Moffit got sick from the stuff and went down to the hospital in Boone, but since she had gotten such a low dose, she recovered quickly. No one else was affected. We suspected that Rob Brannon had been in town that morning because he couldn't stand to be away. He wanted to see the effects of his horrific plan. We never did find him, and he never checked in with his parole officer. He just disappeared.

The Ashe County sheriff caught up with Mary Edith Lumpkin, a.k.a Elphina, in Weavers Ford up by the Virginia border. She was in a car with a young man who seemed to share her vampire fashion sense. Unfortunately for him (as well as Mary Edith), he was going through one of the most famous speed traps in Western North Carolina and the Ashe County sheriff's department tended not to embrace the spiky hair, fishhook-in-the-face look, especially when accompanied by a lot of attitude. Also unfortunately for him, there was a warrant out for Mary Edith's arrest. She admitted the deed when faced with the evidence—Bud's statement, the text messages, the murder weapon—but just shrugged when asked why she'd placed the pumpkin on Flori Cabbage's head. She plead guilty and managed to cut a diminished capacity deal with the D.A. Pauli Girl wasn't surprised.

"I always knew that girl weren't right," Pauli Girl said.

Dave and Collette became an item again, although we rarely saw Collette in St. Germaine. Dave was happy to make the hour drive down the mountain to Wilkesboro to see her, and although they'd been engaged once before, there was no talk about a wedding, at least not to us.

Bud went back to school, got over his heartbreak, and by Christmas was dating another girl, this one, according to Ardine, less toothy.

Kylie Moffit, along with her husband Biff, continued to run Holy Grounds coffee shop, although Kopi Luwak coffee was no longer on the menu.

Marjorie finished her book review for the church newsletter. She was not kind.

The bishop sent us another supply priest until we could hire a new rector. He was a nice fellow who had retired to the mountains from Florida with his wife. With his blessing, we sent the 1928 prayer books back to Lord's Chapel.

Salena Mercer went on to become the biggest seller of vampire fiction of all time, eclipsing even Anne Rice. Her zombie-walk video went viral on YouTube and spurred sales into the millions. She offered to come back to Eden Books on the next Halloween. Georgia politely declined. "It's too nerve-wracking," she said.

Kevin the Zombie ended up choosing not to sue Amelia Godshaw for shooting him in the buttocks with rock-salt. Once his lawyer saw the pictures that Nancy forwarded on to him, the barrister decided that working on contingency, in this case, wasn't going to pay off.

Dr. Ian Burch, PhD, was a man of single-minded intent and once he had his cap set for someone, was determined to win her affections. He continued to add his countertenor to the choir and to woo Tiff St. James to the best of his ability. He even asked me for relationship advice. I referred him to Nancy. Nancy, who still had Flori's laptop, mentioned that she thought she might have discovered the password, and that was the end of it.

Martha Hatteberg never regained her back row seat.

***

Me and Pedro had the coffins looted and were back at the office at 10:06 Eastern Standard Time, which was 7:06 Pacific Time, which if you transpose it, was actually 6:66 PM, not that it mattered to the plot because we were definitely in the prior time zone, but was kinda foreboding nevertheless since Marilyn was sitting primly at her desk when we arrived, her head on backwards, furiously typing sixes.

"You're supposed to be on permanent vacation," I said.

"I heard you were back in business," said Marilyn, spinning her head back around with a sexy shake of her wig and teeth. "How much did you get from those Amish vampires?"

"How did you know we had a case?"

"I have a sense about these things," Marilyn said. "Like the way a beautiful female snake can sense another, even richer snake. The Amish always have gold. They hate banks, you know."

I slung a heavy bag of gold coins onto the desk. It landed with a clunk and a ka-ching. Pedro did the same.

"They had all their coins in their coffins," he said. "Once we got past the Mother Superior, we were home free."

"She didn't whack you with a ruler?"

"Oh, yeah," I said. "We got whacked. Then I got away and Pedro stayed to be whacked a little more."

"What can I say?" remarked Pedro with a grin. "I gotta thing for nuns and it's good to be a detective."

About the Author

Mark Schweizer lives and works in Tryon, North Carolina. He writes books, composes church music, enjoys his granddaughters, works on his cabin, and tends his herd of miniature Himalayan goats.

Okay... Donis said 'no' to the goats.

The Liturgical Mysteries

The Alto Wore Tweed
*Independent Mystery Booksellers Association
"Killer Books" selection, 2004*

The Baritone Wore Chiffon

The Tenor Wore Tapshoes
IMBA 2006 Dilys Award nominee

The Soprano Wore Falsettos
*Southern Independent Booksellers Alliance
2007 Book Award Nominee*

The Bass Wore Scales

The Mezzo Wore Mink

The Diva Wore Diamonds

The Organist Wore Pumps

The Countertenor Wore Garlic

Just A Note

If you've enjoyed this book—or any of the other mysteries in this series—please drop me a line. My e-mail address is mark@sjmp.com. Also, don't forget to visit the website (www.sjmpbooks.com) for lots of great stuff! You'll find recordings and "downloadable" music for many of the now-famous works mentioned in the Liturgical Mysteries including *The Pirate Eucharist, The Weasel Cantata, The Mouldy Cheese Madrigal, Elisha and the Two Bears, The Banjo Kyrie* and a lot more.

Cheers,
Mark